Cowgirls Don't Quit

Susan Carpenter Noble

NEVER QUIT !

Susan Noble

Printed in the United States of America

First Printing May 2020

ISBN 978-1-64871-634-8 Paperback

Published by: Book Services

www.BookServices.us

Contents

Cowgirls Don't Quit

Dedication

This book is dedicated to Jasper Breitenbach, who went on his first cattle drive, eight years ago at age 12, riding his three-year-old filly. It was Jasper who inspired me to write this story. On the cover, Jasper is the rider on the left on his first of many cattle drives.

Cowgirls Don't Quit

Acknowledgments

Thank you to all of the amazing horsemen I was blessed to learn from over the years: Monte Foreman, Bob Allen, Ray Hall, Doug Milholland, Bobby George, and Ward Studebaker. Together these fine horsemen make up the character of Ol' Ben in this book.

Thank you to my family for your encouragement and collective sense of humor.

Thank you to Betsy Hoyt and Michael Feinberg for believing in Meghan and her adventures.

And thank you, dear reader, for coming along for the ride!

Cowgirls Don't Quit

Chapter 1
Meghan Eavesdrops

I had to keep reminding myself to stay quiet, which is something I'm not very good at. With my right hand, I held one branch of the lilac bush aside just far enough that I could see the three people on our front porch. I took a deep breath and hoped the fragrance of the lilacs would calm me down so I could focus on remaining perfectly motionless. Any movement would get me caught and sent back into the house before I could hear my parents' answer. And I knew they wouldn't answer until they asked a bunch of dumb questions the way grown-ups always do.

"Is Meghan a good enough rider to handle something like this?" Dad asked.

Ol' Ben shoved his cowboy hat a little further back on his head and looked up at my very tall father. "Mr. Callahan, that girl is plenty tough enough to help."

I felt myself swelling with pride at his words and had to remind myself yet again to keep still. *Breathe. Smell the lilacs. Keep still!*

"And she'll be ridin' the most experienced cow horse I've got on the place. Rowdy has been helpin' move cattle up to the summer pasture every spring for over twenty years now. Xender rode him the last five years."

I heard the surprise in Mom's voice. "Your grandson has been helping drive cattle since he was six?" she asked.

Ben's eyebrows scrunched together for a second; he looked as if he was figuring something out. "Yes, I guess that'd be about right. He's eleven now, same as your girl."

I am almost twelve, I wanted to shout, but just in time I remembered I didn't want them to know I was there.

"Is Xender helping this year too?" Mom asked.

"Sure is," Ben told her, "but he's got his own horse now. He quit ridin' Rowdy just before you folks moved here. That's one of the reasons I was glad when your little girl was so keen to ride. Rowdy needed a new kid."

I closed my eyes, remembering that day nearly three years ago when my family had followed the moving van down the driveway to the new house outside of Dolores, Colorado. I'd only glanced at the house itself. I was too busy staring at the barn and the corrals that were further back, on the other side of the fence beyond our driveway. I was afraid that if I even blinked, they would vanish. And that would have been terrible. Living on a ranch—or at least next to one, which was practically the same thing—had been my lifelong dream. Well, that and having my own horse someday.

From the day we arrived, I made it my sole purpose in life to watch everything that happened on the ranch. Each day after school I hurried out into the yard with one of my plastic model horses and imitated what I saw Ol' Ben doing. I carefully brushed my precious pony, put on its imaginary saddle, and then exercised it around the back yard, my own ridiculously long legs doing the actual jogging and loping.

One day, as Ol' Ben was riding down the lane to his mailbox, I worked up my courage and walked boldly up to the edge of the yard next to the fence. As he approached, I called out, "That's a pretty horse."

"Well, thank you, young lady. That's a mighty fine lookin' animal you're totin'. What's his name?"

I held up my four-legged treasure and announced, "*Her* name is Ariel Silverbrite."

"Well, she looks like a good one." With that, he closed his mailbox, turned his horse, and headed back up the lane, calling back, "See ya tomorrow."

I excitedly waited for him to show up at his mailbox every day after that, each time with a different plastic horse to show him. Two weeks later, when I was beginning to run low on new horses to introduce, the doorbell rang as my parents and I were finishing dinner.

The old rancher was standing on the front doorstep, cowboy hat in hand. "I'm yer neighbor, Ben," he told Dad, "and it has come to my attention that the young lady there"—he nodded in my direction—"suffers bad from the horse bug. Now it jes' so happens that I've still got the ol' horse that helped teach my kids and grandkids how to ride. And, well, I don't have time to work him these days with all these young horses needin' my attention, so I was thinkin' maybe yer little one would be interested in ridin' him for me. I'll teach her how to get along with him, and she can help with a few chores around the place so's she can learn that there's more to likin' horses than jes' ridin' 'em."

After a few minutes of exchanging names and polite talk, the agreement was made, and I was invited to report Saturday morning for my first lesson on stall cleaning followed by my first lesson on horseback. I went back almost every day after that, weekdays after school and on weekends for as many hours a day as my parents would allow. With all that practice, I could now clean stalls as well as anybody. Even more important, I knew how to brush a real horse and put on a real saddle. And the very best of all: I could climb into that saddle by myself and ride that horse all over Ben's ranch, out through the pastures, down across the Dolores River, and up into the mountains beyond.

I had learned *so* much.

Dad's voice broke into my reverie and brought me back to the present. "Well, Ben, if you really think she can be helpful…"

"And safe," Mom added.

"Then I guess we'll have to let her go along. I know she'll be really excited for the opportunity," Dad concluded.

They almost got to hear how seriously excited I was, but somehow I managed to clamp my mouth shut just in time to keep a shriek of joy penned up inside of me. I let go of the lilac branch, raced around the house to the back door, slipped through it, and ran to my room. I flopped down on top of the pink quilt on my four-poster bed and pretended to be finishing my math assignment. My long, tangly, dark brown hair formed a curtain that hid my face.

Finally Mom tapped on the door frame and walked in.

I continued to stare down at my worksheet, making pencil marks that may or may not have had anything to do with the actual math problem. I knew if I looked up at Mom, the joy and excitement that were bouncing around inside of me would somehow leak out. With tremendous effort, I held my position until Mom shared the "news." Then I jumped off the bed, hugged Mom, and did a happy dance that carried me out of the house, across the yard, and all the way to Ben's barn.

The math could wait. Besides, with school getting out next week for summer vacation, this homework was nothing more than busy work.

Ben was back at the barn already, and I could see short, blonde-headed Xender right behind him.

"From the look on your face, I'm guessing your folks could possibly have mentioned that you *might* be moving cows with us in a couple of weeks," Ben drawled.

The way he said "might" worried me a little bit, but I answered excitedly, "Yes! I can't wait!"

"Well, there's a lot of work to be done betwixt now and then. If you can handle it, we'll be glad to have yer help. If you can't, well, you won't be goin'," Ben responded. "You need to understand: Cowgirls don't quit. An' we only want real cowgirls along."

Xender must have seen my surprise and confusion. He said, "Grandpa told me your folks said yes, but if you turn out to be like Violet, then you can just stay home. She's worthless when we're getting ready. She's afraid she might smudge her makeup or break a nail, so she won't hardly help with the vaccinating or ear-tagging or anything."

I wasn't sure what those things were, but if working at them meant I could go, I was going to amaze them with my efforts. Besides, I'm not in any way, shape, or form like fourteen-year-old Violet. Especially shape. Violet may have been older than me, but she was only five feet tall with a really cute figure, whereas I was at least six inches taller than that, and scrawny. To top it off, Violet had long, straight, perfectly behaved, honey-blonde hair that reached almost to her fancy, western-style leather belt. My hair was out-of-control-wavy. Violet wore tight-fitting blue jeans with bling all over the pockets. My jeans just kind of hung on me and were never quite long enough. Violet wore makeup that was always perfect and made her blue eyes appear to sparkle. My eyes were brown, with a little green in them: "Exactly the color of fresh horse manure," Xender informed me when we were cleaning stalls one day.

There was no doubt about it. Violet and I didn't have much in common.

Out loud, I protested, "I am *not* like your sister!"

"I hope not," Xender and Ol' Ben muttered in stereo.

Cowgirls Don't Quit

Chapter 2
The Adventure Begins

Four o'clock in the morning is really early. I felt as if I had barely slept at all that night, and I probably hadn't. I was too excited to start proving I could be a real cowgirl. Today Ben was taking us over to a ranch about ten miles to the west where we would help vaccinate, ear-tag, and brand the cattle in preparation for their trip up to their summer range in the mountains.

Breakfast, which Mom had insisted on making for me, disappeared off my plate as fast as I could eat it, and I was soon out the door, wearing my cowboy boots, jeans, long-sleeved shirt, sweatshirt, and jacket. It wasn't quite freezing any more in the mornings, but it was pretty cold. The high mountain peaks around us still had snow on them even in late May.

On my head I wore one of Dad's headlamps. He had helped me adjust the straps on it the night before, so that it would shine out in front of me, lighting my way without my having to carry a flashlight. That was good because my hands were already full, carrying my water bottle and the lunch Mom had packed for me.

I took a deep breath of the cold, clean mountain air and turned back to wave goodbye to Mom, as best I could with my armful of stuff.

"I hope you have fun today, sweetie," she called after me. "But be careful!"

"Sure, Mom."

"Are you certain you don't want me to walk over with you?" she asked one last time.

"No, Mom. It's no big deal. Look! The light on the side of Ben's barn is on. All I have to do is aim toward it. It's not as if I'm going to get lost or anything."

"Okay, honey. But be careful," she repeated.

"I will," I promised for the ninety-seventh time that morning.

The light from the headlamp was bright enough that I could see the lane easily. Even so, it was a little freaky being out in the dark by myself. But no way was I going to go back and ask Mom to walk with me. I wasn't about to let Xender start the day off calling me a sissy who needed her mommy because she was afraid of the dark.

Walking toward the barn, I mostly kept my head down, watching for rocks or holes in the dirt road. But once, when I did look up, my headlamp caught the reflection of a greenish-yellow pair of eyes staring at me from the woods beyond the barn. I stopped.

The Adventure Begins

Suddenly the ranch dogs started barking, and I nearly jumped out of my skin. Hearing the dogs must have scared the animal in the woods, because those eyes disappeared. Every few seconds, the eyes would appear again, but each time they were farther away. I took a deep breath of the cool night air and made myself resume walking. This time I only glanced at the road once in a while. Mostly, I scanned the area for any more eyes.

I made it all the way to the barn without seeing any other critters, and I only tripped three or four times on the uneven lane. The familiar smell of hay and leather welcomed me as I walked into the barn, but no people did. Flipping on the light switch, I went into the tack room and stuffed my lunch and water bottle into the saddlebags Ben had strapped on the back of the saddle he lets me use. Still no sign of Xender or Ben.

I grabbed a halter, a lead rope, and a handful of grain, took another deep breath for courage, and headed out into the pasture to catch Rowdy. Latching the gate behind me, I whistled for the horses and made myself start walking out into the grassy field, away from the comforting light of the barn. With each step, I slowly moved my head back and forth, shining the light from the headlamp into the distance and hoping I wouldn't see any more of those scary-looking eyes. Finally, I spotted the horses, about halfway out in the field. Their heads were straight up in the air, and they were blowing and snorting as if something had startled them.

11

Since they were looking straight in my direction, I realized it was me they were afraid of. With the light on my head, I must have looked just as scary to them as those greenish-yellow eyes had to me.

I quickly reached up and fumbled with the switch on the headlamp, finally getting it shut off. While my eyes slowly adjusted to the darkness, I began talking quietly to the horses. I knew it didn't really matter what I said; I just had to use a calm, reassuring tone of voice.

"It's just me, guys. Sorry about that light shining in your eyes. I hate it when people do that to me. But it's okay now. The light's off. It's just me, not some wild animal. And look, I've got a handful of grain for the first horse that comes to me. Come on, Rowdy. You're usually the leader. And besides, I want you to be the one who gets the grain. It's okay, ol' fella. C'mon."

Pretty soon I heard the soft thud of hooves walking across the grass. As I'd hoped, Rowdy was the first to arrive. Even in the starlight, I could see the wide white blaze that ran down the middle of his face. I held my fingers out flat so he could lip the grain out of the palm of my hand without accidentally biting me. While he was focused on getting every last morsel, I used my other hand to put the lead rope over his neck. Once the grain was gone and I could use two hands, I slipped the halter over his head and buckled it.

A big, gangly three-year-old gelding walked up behind me with his nose stretched out.

"Sorry, Freckles, but Rowdy got all the grain. I don't have anything left for you." I rubbed the soft, reddish-brown hair on his neck and scratched him behind his ears as I talked. I made a mental note to bring extra grain next time. I really liked this big colt, with his long legs and curious, friendly eyes, and I was sorry to disappoint him.

Turning back toward Rowdy, I petted him on the neck too. "Let's go, fella," I said, starting toward the gate.

I was proud of myself for going into the dark pasture alone. But, I have to admit, I was really glad to be heading back to the barn now.

Ben and Xender were walking through the gate just as I led Rowdy up to it.

"Well, look who's here," Ben said.

"Better still, look who's right behind her. The whole herd followed her in! We don't have to go out and find them. Cool!" Xender sounded more than a little happy.

"Why?" I asked. "You afraid of the dark?"

"No!" he said, a little too quickly and too loudly, making me pretty certain that I shouldn't believe him.

Xender was carrying two halters. He put one on his buckskin horse and the other on Violet's paint horse.

Meanwhile, Ben caught the big three-year-old, Freckles, who was one of his training horses.

As we led the horses back to the barn, Ben said, "Go ahead and saddle 'em up. But don't put bridles on. Toss yer bridles into the back of the pickup instead." I looked toward the truck and saw that Ben's two Australian Shepherds, Ralph and Rosie, were already in the truck.

We tied the horses to the hitching rack outside of the barn, where the big light shone down. Nailed to the side of the barn was a wire basket that held the curry combs and brushes we used to clean the horses. I brushed Rowdy's reddish-brown coat free of dirt and pulled a few tangles out of his black mane. Then, while Xender and Ben headed for the tack room to grab their saddles, I pulled a hoof pick out of my back pocket and cleaned Rowdy's feet. I was just finishing when Xender and Ben came out of the barn.

"Hey, pokey, what are you waiting for?" Xender asked, sounding annoyed. "If you think someone else is going to saddle your horse for you, you are just plain wrong."

"Leave her alone, Xender," Ben corrected him quietly. "She's the smart one here."

I stuck my tongue out at Xender as I waved the hoof pick at him. Then I turned my back on him and ran into the barn. One of Ben's favorite sayings was, "No hoof; no horse." If your horse went lame because he had a rock stuck in his hoof, you would end up on foot, and I wasn't about to risk that.

Picking up my saddle blanket, I carried it out to where Rowdy stood patiently. After setting it carefully in place on his broad back, I returned for the heavy western saddle. I lugged it up to Rowdy, and with every ounce of strength I had, I heaved the saddle up onto his back, saddlebags and all.

"First try," observed Ben. "You're gettin' a lot stronger, Meghan."

Xender made sure I didn't start feeling too proud of myself by pointing out, "She's saddling the shortest horse on the ranch."

I looked over at him, and he stuck his tongue out at me. I guess that made us even for the day so far.

"Xender, you probably need to saddle Violet's horse for her." Then, shutting off Xender's objections, Ben promised, "I'll make it right for you later."

Since it didn't seem fair that Xender was having to do Violet's work, I helped him by putting the saddle blanket on and by getting her horse's bridle when I brought mine out.

Violet wandered out just as we finished. As always, her hair looked perfect. But her face, despite the makeup, did *not* look perfect. It just looked grumpy.

"You're welcome," Xender said as he untied his sister's horse and handed her the lead rope.

Violet gave him an annoyed look, took the lead rope, and walked toward the horse trailer.

Ben asked, "Have you two got yer brain boxes? Yer folks said you can't go unless you're wearing 'em."

Xender and I both bolted to the barn to grab our riding helmets. By the time we got back, Violet's and Ben's horses were in the trailer, so we loaded ours. Ben closed up the horse trailer and told us to get in the front seat of the club cab truck. Opening the door, we heard a moan of complaint from the back. I looked in that direction and saw Violet curled up on the back seat, one arm flung over her eyes to shield them from the light.

After buckling ourselves in, Xender looked over his shoulder at Violet. He turned back, grinned and reached for the control knob on the radio, turning the volume way up.

Chapter 3
You Can Lead a Horse to Water...

Ben drove us through the still-sleeping town of Dolores, past McPhee Reservoir, and turned west. The sky behind us was getting lighter, and only a few stars remained visible.

Fifteen minutes later, just as the sun started to peek above the eastern horizon, we pulled into the ranch where we were going to be working that day. A man and two teenage boys were saddling their horses.

"That's Mr. Searle and his boys, Cody and Casey," Xender said. He lowered his voice to a whisper. "Those two are probably the only reason Violet decided to come with us today."

Ben stopped the truck and trailer near them and stepped out. While Ben talked to Mr. Searle, Xender threw a crumpled-up piece of paper at Violet's head and jumped out the passenger door. I followed him as fast as I could to get out of harm's way.

After retrieving our bridles from the bed of the truck, we continued to the back of the trailer, where Ben met us to unload the horses. Rowdy, along with Xender's buckskin horse, Scout, calmly stepped out of the trailer as if this was what they did every day. Ben's big sorrel colt leaped out, looking a little sweaty, even though the morning remained cool.

"He seems kind of nervous," I commented to Xender.

"Aw, he's just young and inexperienced. Grandpa will have him quieted down in no time."

The paint horse whinnied from inside the horse trailer. "Violet," Ben commanded, "you get over here and unload your horse." To my surprise, Violet was actually out of the truck. In fact, she was over talking to Cody and Casey. But at the tone in her Grandpa's voice, she came back to the trailer and did as she was told.

We put the bridles on our horses, tightened the girths on their saddles, and mounted up. Ol' Ben's colt calmed down quickly, just as Xender had predicted.

I wasn't sure what I was supposed to be doing, so when Ben, Xender, Violet, Cody, Casey, and Ben's two dogs headed toward the gate that Mr. Searle was holding open, I followed along.

Ben stopped his young horse and waited for me to catch up with him. It was time for a lesson.

"There are about eighty cow-calf pairs in this pasture. We're goin' to herd 'em into that pen over there and separate the cows from their calves so we can do some vaccinatin' and ear-taggin' and the like," Ben said. I hoped I wasn't supposed to know exactly what he meant because I still didn't.

Before I could ask any questions, Ol' Ben continued, "You're ridin' the most experienced cow horse here, Meghan, so I think you're goin' to have some real fun today when it comes time to separate 'em. First though, we're just goin' to ride real quiet-like around the herd and bring them back to the corral. So for the next half hour, I don't want to see anyone goin' faster than a walk." He turned toward his granddaughter and asked, "Did you hear that, Violet?"

"Yes, Grandpa." From the tone of her voice, I suspect she was rolling her eyes as she spoke.

"The main thing, Meghan, is don't crowd the cattle. We don't want any of the calves gettin' scared and running into—or through—the fence. So stay back a ways. Be ready, though, if any of 'em turn back and try to run past you. You'll need to grab ahold of the saddle horn 'cause Rowdy's *not* goin' to let 'em get by him. You won't have to do anything except hold on." Ben chuckled. "But you'll have to do that real well."

Violet actually laughed. "Yeah. Rowdy stuck Xender's head in the dirt a couple years ago when a calf turned back," she remarked.

Xender's face turned red. "I'd like to see *you* stay on him when he does that with no warning." He turned away from his sister and informed me, "Rowdy was the state champion cutting horse when he was younger.

19

Grandpa raised him and trained him, and they won the title two years in a row!"

I knew Rowdy was a neat horse, but wow, he was practically royalty!

We circled around behind the cattle and then began walking slowly toward them. Ben told Violet and me to stay in the middle, near him, while he sent the two teenage boys to the far side of the herd. He told Xender to take the two dogs, Ralph and Rosie, over to the opposite outside edge. Gradually, we crowded the cows and their calves into a group and headed them back toward the pens near the gate.

Ben reminded me to keep my reins loose and, if I needed to steer Rowdy, to use my legs. But I didn't need to do anything. Rowdy was always exactly where he was supposed to be. Ben sometimes had to remind the others to "move up" or "quit crowdin' 'em," but he never had to say anything to Rowdy and me.

I watched carefully to see if any of the cows might try to turn back. Even though I didn't see any of them looking as if they were going to, I kept one hand near the saddle horn, just in case.

Slowly, we moved the cattle across the field toward a large pen in the corner of the pasture. Mr. Searle had the wide, double gates swung open, and we aimed the cattle toward it. We slowed down to almost a crawl and let the cows and their calves file through.

Cody and Casey jumped off their horses and helped their dad shut the gates before any of the cows came back out.

"That was the easy part," said Xender. "Now we have to separate the cows into a different pen without letting the calves get through."

I looked toward Ben for instructions. He explained, "This is where you and Rowdy are going to earn yer keep. You're goin' to push the mommas through the gate that Cody is working and send the calves over toward that side of the pen, where Xender and I will keep 'em bunched up. Keep yer reins loose so you're not messin' him up. Other than that, just be sure you keep Rowdy between you and the ground."

Violet laughed again. She was looking at me. Something about the expression on her face made me think she was expecting to see me get *my* head stuck in the dirt today.

Once again, Rowdy knew his job, and this time I wasn't holding the saddle horn 'just in case.' I was holding on because I needed to! He would jump back and forth so fast, getting between a cow and her calf, that everything was a blur. But somehow, I managed to stay in the saddle.

As the sun rose higher against a beautiful, clear blue sky, we shed our jackets and sweatshirts. By mid-morning, I was hot, dusty, sweaty, thirsty, and my face hurt from smiling. I was starting to get the hang of it, and the world wasn't spinning so much now. I could actually watch the calves and anticipate where Rowdy was going to turn next!

Once the cows and calves were in separate pens, Mr. Searle finally suggested we stop for a drink of water. I stepped down off Rowdy and opened my saddlebag. The water in the bottle was still cool and tasted wonderful. Seeing an apple in the bag, I pulled it out and started munching on it.

Rowdy smelled it and turned his head to look at me hopefully.

"I'll share, fella, but you have to wait 'til I get more than one little bite." Before long, I couldn't resist those big brown eyes, and I handed him the rest of my apple.

Then it occurred to me that if I was thirsty, he must be, too. Ben saw me pull a water bucket out of the back of the truck and said, "Good idea, Meghan, but let's water 'em the easy way. Climb up on yer horse and follow me. Xender, how 'bout if you untie Violet's horse and bring him along?" Violet was too busy watching Casey and Cody practicing their roping skills to take care of her horse.

We followed Ben to where a small stream cut through the corner of the pasture. Ben's young horse stopped when he got a few feet from the edge of the water. He clearly did not want to get any closer.

"You kids take yer horses in."

Good ol' Rowdy walked past Ben's colt, stepped into the edge of the creek and plunged his nose into the clear water. Xender, on the downstream side, took another few steps past me so his two horses could drink water that hadn't been stirred up by Rowdy's hooves.

I turned in the saddle to look back at Ben who was still encouraging Freckles to follow our horses in.

After another moment's hesitation, the big four-legged youngster finally stepped into the water. He sniffed at it, but then he raised his head without drinking any.

"Why didn't he want to walk into the stream?" I asked. "He goes through the one in your pasture all the time."

"This looks different to him," Ben explained. "Freckles may be big, but he's still a colt. He needs more experiences like this in different places. It's all part of the learnin' process."

I watched the young horse as he continued to look around. He had a white snip on his nose and a big white diamond-shape on his forehead between his huge, brown eyes.

"Why won't he drink?" I asked.

"Well," Ben said, "that's another learnin' thing. This water probably smells different than he's used to. Once he gets thirsty enough, he won't be so persnickety." I now understood the old saying, "You can lead a horse to water, but you can't make him drink."

The other horses had quenched their thirst, and Freckles still wasn't showing any inclination to drink from the stream, so we turned and headed back to the corrals.

"Now that the cows and calves are separated, we're going to run 'em all through a squeeze chute, one at a time. We'll vaccinate the mommas and then brand and vaccinate the little ones," Ben was explaining. "I think it would be best if—"

Ben's voice was cut off by shouting and screaming from the direction of the corral. The shouting voices were those of the boys. The screaming was Violet's.

Chapter 4
Vaccination Time

One of the boys was yelling, "Turn him away from your rope!"

Whatever Violet was screaming in response wasn't intelligible.

It was difficult to tell exactly what was going on, but in the middle of a cloud of dust, I could see Violet riding Cody's—or maybe it was Casey's—horse. The horse had his tail clamped down tightly and was bucking. Violet was grabbing for the saddle horn with one hand. Her other hand held tightly to a lariat that appeared to wrap back behind her and under the horse's tail. From there, it went in the direction of a calf who was pulling as hard as he could to get loose.

"Violet," Ben's voice boomed, "turn loose of the rope and turn that horse toward me."

Maybe because she was used to reacting to her grandfather's voice, Violet was finally able to do what she needed to do. Within seconds the rope was out from under the horse's tail, and he stopped bucking. Meanwhile, the calf trotted across the pen, dragging the lariat behind him.

Very calmly, as if seeing someone nearly get bucked off a horse was no more exciting than watching a cow swat her tail at a fly, Ben said, "One of you boys go get that rope back. And Violet, you come get your own horse and tie him up for the afternoon. Then grab a pen out of the truck so you can take notes for Mr. Searle."

Violet stepped down off the horse's back and handed the reins to Cody. Then she walked shakily across the pen, climbed the fence, and took her horse from her brother.

"Pretty dumb to let a calf get behind you once you've roped him," Xender observed.

Violet scowled. "At least I managed to rope him, which is more than you can do most of the time."

Xender countered. "You haven't seen me rope in a while. I'm getting good."

"You couldn't have gotten much worse."

Xender ignored the barb. "Next rodeo, you ought to try a new event, Violet. I mean, I wouldn't want you to waste your money on roping or anything like that, but I think you've got a promising future as a bronc rider. Though we may have to put some duct tape over your mouth for the event 'cause judges don't award extra points for screaming."

26

"You're just jealous because I can stay on when a horse does something more than a slow walk," she snarled as she turned and walked away.

Ben rode over next to us. "If you're done tormentin' yer sister, how 'bout tying yer horse up and helpin' Mr. Searle set up the vaccination table?"

"But, Grandpa—"

"You'll get a chance later," Ben cut him off. "Right now, I need you on the ground, helpin' Mr. Searle."

Ben turned to me. "You too, Meghan. Go tie Rowdy up and loosen his girth for a while. He worked hard all morning, and he needs a break. Mr. Searle will show you what to do when you get back from tendin' to yer horse."

We all had jobs to do. Ben would use his big colt to crowd the momma cows into the chute. Xender would then shut the back gate behind them, and Casey would work the curved front gate so that it closed around the cow's neck, trapping her in the narrow chute. Then Cody would pour an insecticide on the cow's back that Ben told me would help protect her for a few months from lice and flies. Meanwhile, Casey would read the number on each cow's ear tag to Violet, who would write down the number along with whatever other information Mr. Searle told her.

My job was to fill a disposable syringe with what was called an eight-way vaccination and hand it to Mr. Searle, who would give each cow her shot. He showed me how to stick the tip of a needle through the rubber stopper in the bottle and blow a syringe-full of air into the bottle. Then I would tip the bottle up and pull the plunger back on the syringe, filling it to the correct level. I felt kind of awkward at first, but after a dozen or so, I got faster at it. I'd hand him the syringe, he would administer the shot, and then throw it into a big, empty bucket while I prepared the next one.

A few times, we had to stop because a cow's ear tag was missing, damaged, or unreadable and Casey would have to make a new one. To put it in the cow's ear, he used a special tool that looked sort of like a pair of pliers.

Casey saw me watching him and asked, "Do you want your ears pierced, too? Just come over here and I'll fix you right up."

Everyone else laughed. I hadn't thought about it before, but I guess ear-tagging is basically ear-piercing for cows.

We had a few dozen cows left to vaccinate when Mr. Searle dropped an empty syringe before he could throw it into the bucket. He picked it up and dropped it again.

"Is your arm starting to hurt, Dad?" Casey asked.

"I'm not sure 'starting' is the correct term," Mr. Searle said. Turning to me, he said, "Young lady, I think you're about to get a promotion from shot-preparer to shot-giver."

My stomach suddenly started churning uncomfortably. I didn't want to give a cow a shot. I hated *getting* shots. The last time our family doctor had given me one, I thought I was going to pass out. But then I remembered what Ben had said a few days ago: "There's a lot of work to be done betwixt now and then. If you can handle it, we'll be glad to have yer help. If you can't, you won't be goin'. You need to understand: Cowgirls don't quit. An' we only want real cowgirls along."

I gritted my teeth. I was determined to go on the big cattle drive. "Sure," I said. "I can do this." Me, who was terrified of getting shots, was now going to give them.

"Thank you, Meghan. I only got my arm out of a cast yesterday, and it just isn't back to full strength yet." Mr. Searle rubbed his sore arm. "Okay, then, you've watched me vaccinate fifty-six cows so far. Tell me what you know."

"Well, I saw that you thumped the cow on the neck two or three times and then stuck the needle in. Just the needle, without the syringe attached to it. Umm… why do you thump them like that first?"

"Well, if you just jab the needle in without warning, they usually try to jerk away pretty hard, which of course they can't really do in this chute. But if you thump 'em a few times, first lightly, then harder, then harder again before you stick the needle in, they don't get too upset. No sense upsetting 'em 'cause if they get mad and start thrashing around, even in the chute, they might hurt themselves or somebody else. Got it?"

"Got it!" I nodded and concentrated. "Then you attached the syringe, and, well, it sort of looked like

29

you were pulling the plunger back first before you pushed it in to actually give the shot."

"Very observant! That's exactly what I was doing. These vaccines are meant to go into the muscles. If I accidentally stick the needle into a vein and give the shot, it could kill her. When I pull back, if I see blood in the syringe, I know I've hit a vein, so I have to pull the needle out and put it in another spot." He paused as if he was waiting for me to say something.

"Okay." I paused again, thinking. "Then after you pulled the needle out, you always rubbed the area where you gave the shot."

"Yep. Makes 'em feel better. Just like when I rub my sore arm."

"Okay."

"Well, don't just stand there, Meghan. We're burnin' daylight. Go vaccinate that cow," Ben hollered from the cattle pen.

"Cowgirls don't quit, cowgirls don't quit," I repeated silently as I walked over to the cow and thumped her tentatively with the back of my hand.

"The last couple of hits need to be harder," Mr. Searle advised.

I thumped a few more times, harder.

"That's better. Now stick that needle in her neck like you mean it."

I tried, but I felt myself chickening out at the last second, and the needle only went about halfway in.

30

"Pull it out and start again in a new spot," he told me, "and don't be such a wuss about it."

This time I thumped harder and then drove the needle home into her neck muscle. I was simultaneously proud of getting it right on only my second try and also freaked out that I had done it at all.

Casey grumbled, "What are you waiting for? Stick the syringe on that needle and give her the shot. We've got a lot a cows waiting while you're wasting time admiring your work."

While I fumbled with the syringe, Mr. Searle reminded me, "Don't forget to pull back and look for blood before you shoot it." I pulled, but nothing happened. Mr. Searle nodded to me and I pushed the plunger in. Then I pulled out the needle and rubbed the cow's neck.

Casey jerked open the headgate and the cow walked out, mooing and looking for her baby, who was in the other pen.

Xender opened the back gate, and the next cow in line stepped into the chute, probably thinking she could walk straight through with the cow who was just leaving. But Casey's timing was good; he shut the headgate exactly in time to stop her. At the same instant, Xender closed the gate behind her so she couldn't back out.

On my next attempt, I had a better idea how much pressure to use, and I was able to get the needle in on the first try. At first, I had to think carefully about each step of the process, but gradually I started to feel a little more confident. Even so, I was really glad when the last cow was safely through the chute.

Mr. Searle called for a lunch break about then. Ben tied up his young horse while the rest of us dug out our lunches, walked over to a clump of cottonwood trees, and found some shade to sit in. Any need for sweatshirts or jackets was long gone. The sun was beating down from a cloudless sky.

After I finished my sandwich, I leaned back against the trunk of the tree and watched the cattle milling about in the pens. "What happens this afternoon?" I wondered aloud.

Cody was the quickest to answer. "We'll run most of the calves through the chute, one at a time, just like the cows. You'll give each of 'em a shot while I brand 'em. Most of 'em already have ear tags 'cause we usually ear-tag within a week of birth."

"If they have ear tags, why do they have to be branded too?" I asked.

Cody gave me a condescending look. "You are such a greenhorn."

When Cody didn't offer any further explanation, Xender told me, "It's because they're all going up to their summer range on Taylor Mesa. When we move them up there next week, they'll be sharing the range with cattle from other ranches. Next Fall, we'll have to sort them out, and it will be easier to look at the brands than the ear tags. Besides, some of the numbers on the ear tags might be the same as calves from other ranches. Mr. Searle here has a cow #142, but one of the other ranches probably has a cow with that same number."

"I can see where that would get confusing."

Xender got a far-away look in his eyes. "When I grow up, my brand is going to have an XYZ in it, just like my initials: Xender Yale Zimmerman," he said proudly.

Cody started laughing. "Your middle name is Yale?"

"I can just see it: 'XYZ Ranch, end of the alphabet, end of the line,'" said Casey.

Violet joined in. "It'll have to be the *Lazy* XYZ ranch if Xender owns it."

"Only if you're one of the partners in my ranch. Which you *won't* be!" declared Xender.

Mr. Searle shut down the dispute by standing up and asking, "You okay with giving more shots this afternoon, Meghan?"

"Yes sir, I am," I replied, conscious of the fact that Ben was looking at me.

"Well, I appreciate that. I surely do," Mr. Searle said. Then turning to Xender, he asked, "You willing to help Cody move the calves? One of you can work the back gate of the chute for a while, and the other can move the cows on horseback; then you can trade off. And when it comes time to rope and stretch the ones we have to tag and brand, you can be Cody's header."

"Yes, sir! That'll be fine with me!"

"Xender's going to be the header? We'll never get done," Violet complained.

Everyone ignored her.

"I can handle the front gate of the chute," said Ben, "and Violet will continue to take notes, unless she would prefer to trade jobs with Meghan or me."

The look on Violet's face said she wasn't happy with any of the choices, but she was smart enough not to pitch a fit. "I'll keep taking the notes," she said, scuffing the toes of her boots in the dirt.

"Let's get to work then. Casey, go light the propane tank and start heating the branding irons."

Chapter 5
The Stranger

The calves weren't always cooperative about loading into the chutes, but as soon as one was in place, I would give the shot, and Casey would brand his or her hip. When we let the calf out, it would trot into the herd of cows, happy to find its momma.

Finally, after what seemed like hours, Cody called out, "That's the last of the ear-tagged calves. We've got eight left for Xender and me to rope."

Xender yelled, "Yippee!" and ran to untie his horse. Once he was mounted up, he shook out his lariat, forming a big loop at the end of the rope. He rode his horse slowly toward the eight remaining calves.

"Have you got the next syringe ready?" Casey asked me.

"Yeah," I said, not taking my eyes off the two riders.

"Good. Be ready to follow Ben and me in when the time comes."

I wasn't sure how this was supposed to work, but I figured if he and Ben started to move, I would be right behind them.

Xender swung his loop, threw perfectly, and watched it settle down over the neck of one of the calves. He pulled the slack out so the loop tightened down like a dog collar around the calf's neck. Then he turned his horse and pulled the calf away from the little herd. The calf took only a couple of steps before Cody's lariat looped down and caught the calf's hind feet. Cody pulled tight while turning his horse away.

"Nicely done, boys," said Ben as he and Casey started toward the calf, who was getting stretched in two different directions by the pull of the ropes. Ben and Casey grabbed him and helped lay him down on the ground.

"Meghan come sit down—kinda straddle him across his shoulders," Ben yelled as he helped hold the calf's head down.

I did as I was told and was able to give the calf his shot.

"Now hop off and go get the next syringe while we finish up."

As soon as I was on my feet, Casey sat down over the calf, facing in the opposite direction. With Casey in place, holding the calf down, Ben ear-tagged the calf. Then I noticed that Casey was holding a tool that had what looked like a heavy-duty rubber band on one end of it. I watched as Casey leaned toward the calf's underbelly, back by his hind legs, with the tool.

Ben, who had gone to get the branding iron, walked past me just then.

"We used to use a knife to castrate the bull calves. These elastic bands make it easier. It's not so painful, and there's no danger of infection," Ben said. "Mr. Searle and the boys got the rest of 'em done when the calves were just a few days old, so we've jes' got these few young 'uns left to do."

As soon as they put the brand on the calf's hip, they pulled the ropes off and let him up. Cody and Xender recoiled their ropes and had the next calf roped and stretched in no time. I gave the shot and Ben ear-tagged, but this time Casey showed up with the branding iron.

"No rubber band this time?" I asked.

Casey laughed. "This one's a heifer," he said, as if that explained everything.

"It's a girl calf," Ben clarified.

Usually we didn't have to wait too long for Cody and Xender to rope the next calf, but the final calf was a real escape artist; the two boys had a terrible time getting their ropes on her. But at last they got her caught and we finished.

"Either that little heifer is going to grow up to be one of the herd leaders or else she'll jes' plain be trouble," said Ben. Looking toward Violet, he quietly added, "Kinda like someone else here today."

Once those last few calves were turned into the pen with the cows and had "mothered up," as Mr. Searle called it, the constant mooing and bawling we had been listening to all day eased up. It was suddenly almost quiet, which made it easy, from where I stood, to hear Violet complaining to Casey.

"Why should she have all the fun, while I got stuck being the stupid secretary? Next time, *she* can stand there writing notes all day and being bored out of her mind," Violet said petulantly.

"I thought you didn't like vaccinating," ventured Casey.

"I don't. It's gross. But standing around writing stuff all day isn't any fun either." Her tone of voice suddenly turned sweet. "Fix it with your dad so I don't have to do any of the boring, dirty stuff next time, Casey."

Casey actually laughed. "It'd be okay with me if you just hung around looking pretty all day, but face it, Violet, even if my dad was okay with that, your Grandpa would never agree."

Violet's voice went back to its previous, whiney tone. "Why does he have to be so mean to me all the time?"

I could not believe she had just said that. Ben was always cutting her slack. Xender and I were the ones who got up extra early this morning to help Ben get the horses ready. Xender had even watered her horse while Violet hung out with the boys at midmorning. In fact, even now, he was untying her horse to do so again. How could she be so unfair?

"You coming, Meghan?" Xender's voice broke into my thoughts. I ran over to where Rowdy was tied, put his bridle back on, tightened the girth, and mounted up. Ben, Xender—riding his own horse while leading Violet's—and I rode back across the field to the watering hole. This time Ben's big colt was the first one into the little stream and started drinking after only a quick sniff.

"He's a smart one," Ben commented. "It takes some of 'em a lot longer than one day to catch on."

I smiled. I liked hearing that the big red colt was smart.

As we headed back toward the horse trailer to load up, Ben said, "I'm real proud of you two. You both worked hard all day. We've got two more days like this at two more ranches before we'll be ready to move the cattle. And we'll have bigger herds the next two days. You up for that?"

"Yes sir!" Xender and I answered in chorus.

"I wish some of your attitude would rub off on Violet," he said quietly. Then more forcefully, he went on, "Just make sure it doesn't go the other direction."

Violet didn't go the next day. She "wasn't feeling well," Xender told me in a mocking tone. But there was plenty of help at the second ranch already, so we didn't need her or the help of a man with a bristly, gray beard who showed up looking for work that morning. He walked up to the owner of the ranch and asked in a raspy, not-very-nice-sounding voice if he'd like to hire a "top cowhand" for his crew. The owner shook his head and politely but emphatically said he already had plenty of good workers before turning his back on the man.

The stranger didn't leave right away, but tried to strike up a conversation with some of the other people who were helping. No one seemed too interested in talking with him, and he finally climbed back into his old truck and left.

I felt an odd sense of relief when he'd gone. Something about him had made me uneasy, though I wasn't sure exactly what it was. He had been dressed in dirty blue jeans and an old, worn shirt. That's how most of us on the work crew were dressed, so that wasn't it. I hadn't liked his voice. But that seemed unfair, and I felt a little guilty about holding the sound of his voice against him. I mean, he probably didn't like sounding that way any more than I liked hearing him.

I was still thinking about my reaction when I heard some of the adults talking.

"Who was that anyway? He looked familiar."

"Name's Hillman, or Hillson, or something like that. Haven't seen him around here in years."

"That's right. Hillson. Now I remember! He used to work down at the livestock auction, but they fired him for embezzling money."

I looked over at Xender, who was listening to the men too. His eyes were huge, probably a lot like mine. We had just been standing next to a criminal! I didn't feel so guilty about not liking him or his voice anymore.

Before long we got busy and thoughts of seeing a real, live criminal were replaced by the necessity of having to focus on my job.

Xender and I got to go along with Ben to gather the cows out of the winter pasture, and Rowdy and I got to take a turn at separating the mommas from the calves. But Xender didn't get to do any roping. Mostly we spent the afternoon running errands for the adults. They called us "go-fers," as in "go fer a drink of water," or "go fer a fresh jar of vaccine from the cooler in the truck," or "go fer a new bag of ear tags."

By the next day, Violet was "all better" and came along with us. At this ranch, unlike yesterday's, there were several teen-age boys on the work crew. Now I understood what Xender had meant yesterday when he said Violet had gotten a case of 'no-boy-itis.'

The good thing at this third ranch was that there were enough teens and adults to fill most of the jobs, but not enough that Xender and I got left out. It was a great day! We both helped round up and then separate the cattle; Xender was able to do some of the roping, and I filled in on vaccination duty when someone else needed a rest. A couple of the adults who hadn't been with us at either of the other ranches, looked surprised when I stepped up and started vaccinating. Ben just looked proud.

Violet ended up being the go-fer that day, which seemed to suit her fine. She didn't have to get too dirty and only complained a little about being bored.

On the way back to the ranch, I asked, "There were three cows and their calves today who were all white, and I was wondering... um, my teacher had some albino rats in the classroom last year. Is that what those cows were? Albinos?"

"Good question, Meghan," Ben said. He got quiet for a minute as he often did before answering anything that he deemed a 'good question.' Finally he continued, "Albino animals have pink skin and usually blue eyes. Did you notice what color skin those cows had?"

"Well, I got to vaccinate them and, um, I'd have to say their eyes were brown and their skin was dark, like all the others."

"That's right. That's 'cause they're not albinos. They're a breed called Charolais cattle, and one of the characteristics of that breed is a creamy-colored coat." Ben chuckled. "It sure makes it easy to pick 'em out in a crowd, doesn't it?"

"It sure does," I agreed. The other cows were mostly black or reddish-brown, and a few were tan. But those creamy white cows really stood out.

As we pulled into the driveway at Ben's ranch, he changed the subject. "You three can sleep in a little

42

tomorrow, but don't get used to it. We'll be startin' out on the cattle drive the day after."

He said, "We!" That must mean I was going to be allowed to go too!

Chapter 6
The Drive Begins

This time I had extra grain in my jacket pocket, because I always felt guilty giving only one horse a treat. The moon, which wasn't quite full, was hanging low on the western horizon. The glow made the stars seem less bright, but it also made it easier to see the horses silhouetted in the pasture. I walked out into the field to catch Rowdy and was surprised when he wasn't the first horse to come when I called. Ben's training horse, Freckles, beat the rest of the herd. I gave the big colt a handful of grain, then reached in my pocket for more when Rowdy showed up. Freckles tried to get it, too, but Rowdy flattened his ears and bared his teeth toward the young horse, who got the message and backed off. I slipped the halter over Rowdy's head, fed him a second handful of grain, and told him what a good boy he was.

"I can't believe how willing you are, old boy. You come every morning when I call, even though you know when I'm here in the dark like this, you're going to have a long day."

Rowdy pushed me with his nose. If he could talk, I think he would have been saying, "Well, if it's going to be a long day, let's get started."

I led him out of the pasture and tied him to the hitching rack under the light. Ben, Xender, and Violet hadn't arrived yet, which was probably because I was fifteen minutes earlier than normal. I'd woken up before my 4:00 a.m. alarm went off and was too excited to go back to sleep.

Freckles nickered softly from the pasture. I grabbed another halter and went over to catch him too. While he munched on the handful of grain that I gave him, I buckled the halter around his large head. "Ben says you're going to have to grow some more to catch up with that head. But that's okay. You're like me. We're the youngest ones on the ranch but we're the tallest, aren't we, Freckles?"

I eased him through the pasture gate and took him to the hitching rack. Still no sign of the others, so I grabbed two more halters and went back for Xender's and Violet's horses. Then I cleaned Rowdy's feet and started brushing him. When I was carrying the saddle blanket out of the tack room, the rest of them finally showed up.

"Look who's anxious to go on her first cattle drive," said Ben with a grin.

"Thanks for catching the horses," said Xender.

The Drive Begins

"Feh," muttered Violet, underwhelmed.

While we saddled our horses, Ben announced, "If you don't have rain gear, food, and water in yer saddlebags, deal with that problem right now 'cause later on you'll be flat outta luck. And put your helmets in the truck, or you'll find yourself walkin' all day. You too, Violet."

Violet opened her mouth to respond, but Ben continued without a pause, "And don't waste yer breath telling me it'll mess up yer hair. We're gonna be on the highway today, and even your hard head would lose an argument with concrete if you landed on it."

Once we had the horses loaded up, we drove to the farthest of the three ranches where we had been helping during the past week. The cattle were all in the pens, so as soon as we unloaded our horses, bridled them, and mounted up, we were ready to go. Ben handed his truck keys to the rancher's wife, Mrs. Carlton, who drove out onto the dirt road.

"She'll be leading the drive in Grandpa's rig," Xender explained. "That doesn't matter much on these dirt roads, but when we turn onto the highway, we have to have someone out in front flagging down oncoming traffic."

Ben rode up next to us. "We'll pick up a few more riders, along with a lot more cows, at the next two ranches so our positions may change throughout the day. But for now, Violet and I are going to ride alongside the middle of the herd and try to keep 'em from turning off into driveways or crossroads. Mr. Carlton and his hired man will take the lead, and you two are going to ride drag. I hope you remembered yer bandannas 'cause you're gonna want something over yer face when this herd starts stirrin' up the dust. If you have any questions today, Meghan, you can ask any of the other riders. They've all been doing this for years."

"Okay," I said. I turned toward Xender and opened my mouth, but before I could say a word, he answered.

"Riding drag means we follow behind the cattle, keeping them moving and making sure none of them gets left behind."

The cattle began pouring out of the pen onto the road. I noticed Xender was putting a bandanna over his mouth, so I got mine out and did the same. We looked like bandits, I thought, and giggled behind my mask.

Among the last of the cattle to come out of the pen were the three Charolais cows and their calves. With all the dust the cows were stirring up, I wondered if they would still look all creamy-white by this evening.

Xender and I moved into place behind them. The cows walked or trotted along, their babies cavorting beside them.

"They look as if they're excited to go too!" I exclaimed.

"Most of the mommas have made this trip before. They're looking forward to the spring grass they'll be eating on the mesa, so yeah, they probably are kind of excited now. But it's going to be a long day for them.

And it's really going to be long for the calves. They should be fine for a while, but we need to keep an eye on the youngest ones. Any that get too tired, we can put into one of the trailers."

"*One* of the trailers?" I asked. "There's only one."

"Mr. Searle will be driving a truck and stock trailer too. He'll be at the back of the herd to keep traffic from coming up on us too fast from behind once we're out on the highway."

As we approached the next ranch, I saw more cattle coming out of a pen and joining our group. I remembered that there were about 150 cow-calf pairs at that ranch. Including the herd we started with, we now had 270 pairs, and we would soon be picking up another 80 from Mr. Searle's ranch. That was going to be a lot of animals to keep watch over.

I patted Rowdy on the neck. "I'm glad you know what you're doing, fella."

For the first mile, while we collected the three herds, it was a little dusty, but not too miserable with the bandannas over our faces. The herd was moving along at a pretty good pace in the cool morning air, so sometimes we had to jog to keep up. Mostly I was watching the cattle, but once, I saw movement out of the corner of my eye in a hayfield as we passed by. I glanced that way and saw a fox trotting along parallel to us.

"Xender! Look!" I yelled as I pointed toward the wild creature.

Xender looked. "He's been with us for the past quarter of a mile. Did you only just see him?" He laughed at me. "Some lookout you are."

I ignored his dismissive tone. "What should we do?"

"Nothing. He's not going to bother us. He's too little to be a threat, even to the smallest calves. Besides, Grandpa's dogs are keeping an eye on him. If he gets near any of the calves, Ralph and Rosie will run him off."

I believed him, but I kept watching the fox just the same. I had never gotten to study a fox this close up for this long. His reddish-brown fur looked a little tattered, probably because he was still shedding out his winter coat. From the bottom of his chin all the way down between his front legs, his chest was covered in white fur, and his legs were black. His long thin nose and pointy ears were tipped in black, while his big bushy tail was a mixture of red and black, except for the last little bit of it, which was white. In the early morning light, he almost didn't look real.

Once in a while, he stopped to sniff at something. Finally, he stopped and crouched down for a full minute. Suddenly, he pounced. Whatever he was hunting, probably a prairie dog, he must have gotten, because he scooped something up in his mouth and trotted away from us.

Prairie dogs are cute, so I kinda felt sorry for it. On the other hand, foxes have to eat too. Besides, prairie dogs dig a lot of holes in the fields. One of Ben's friends, who had a ranch south of town, lost a horse

last summer when it stepped in a prairie dog hole and broke its leg. I had cried when I heard about that.

Before I could think any more about it, the three Charolais cows and their calves peeled away from the herd and started down a side road. Rowdy sprung into action, and I shoved my weight down into my heels so I wouldn't end up in the dirt. I also grabbed the saddle horn because I didn't want to accidentally pull on the reins. Rowdy needed his head free to be able to do his work.

We circled around the cows at a lope, got in front of them and made them turn back toward the herd. Once he had them going in the right direction, Rowdy slowed back down.

"What a good boy, Rowdy. You're not even crowding them," I rubbed his neck and praised him. Once they were back on the road and saw the rest of the herd in front of them, the cows picked up a trot and re-joined the herd.

Rowdy and I jogged along behind them. Xender pulled his bandanna down around his neck, grinned at me from the other side of the road and gave me a thumbs up.

This was so cool! I was actually on a cattle drive and with Rowdy's help, I was being a real cowgirl!

Cowgirls Don't Quit

Chapter 7
On the Highway with the Herd

Up ahead, the front of the herd was coming up on the Searle Ranch. Casey and Cody and their two dogs drove their cattle out onto the road, and our numbers were complete. In another quarter mile, we'd be off the dirt road and onto the highway.

"Where's Mr. Searle?" I asked Xender as we rode past the gate to the Searle Ranch. "I thought he was supposed to follow us."

"He will," Xender explained. "But his first job is to get out ahead of the herd and block the highway so we can move the herd onto the road without traffic problems. See? There he is up ahead."

I looked through the dust and saw that the front of the herd was turning onto the paved road. Mr. Searle's truck and stock trailer were behind them, and Ben's rig, with Mrs. Carlton driving, was creeping along the highway ahead of them. It was early enough in the morning that traffic wasn't too heavy yet, although a few cars and trucks were coming to a stop from both directions.

We, too, finally reached the highway and followed the last few cows onto it. It was comical watching the calves when they came to the striped line down the middle of the pavement. Many of them stopped and looked at it before jumping over it. I don't think I'd ever seen a cow jump before.

The herd was crowded onto one side of the highway. Some were on the road itself, but most were off in the grass and weeds between the pavement and the fence that ran alongside the field next to it. The fence ran in an unbroken line for quite a distance. That meant Rowdy and I shouldn't have to worry about cows trying to take any more side trips for a while. I pulled my bandanna down around my neck and took a deep breath. Now that we were off the dirt road, I didn't need it anymore.

Xender was up on the highway helping keep the cows over on the right side. Oncoming traffic could still safely get through in the other lane if they drove past slowly, though once in a while a few of the cows would drift across the center line, forcing the drivers to stop or swerve.

When there was a break in the oncoming traffic, either Xender or Mr. Searle, who was now following us in Ben's truck, would signal the vehicles behind us to pull around and begin the process of passing the herd. The drivers were being sensible, easing past us slowly, and everything was going well.

On the Highway with the Herd

A huge RV with California license plates came along and began to thread its way past the herd. It was fun to watch because the kids in the RV were pressing their noses against the windows to see the cows. They were even using their cellphones to take pictures, both of the cows and of us. It made me feel like a celebrity.

After about a mile and a half on the highway, we turned east onto another paved, two-lane road. This one didn't get as much traffic as the one we had just turned off, but it had a lot more places where the cows could go astray: more driveways and crossroads. I was going to have to start watching the cows more carefully.

Ben, who was farther ahead of us on Xender's side had stopped and was standing his horse in the middle of a wide driveway. When the front and middle parts of the herd had passed it, Xender crossed over onto the shoulder of the road and loped up to Ben. As soon as Xender got there, Ben took off at a lope to catch up to the front of the herd, where he took over from Casey, who was standing guard at another driveway. It looked as if they were playing musical chairs on horseback.

Wondering if I would have to do that, I looked ahead on my side of the road. But once again, a fence stretched alongside for as far as I could see. The only thing I had to do was make sure the cows kept moving, and they seemed to be doing that pretty well on their own.

Since everything was going well, I let my mind and my eyes wander. Off in the distance to my right, I could see a long mesa stretching across the southeastern horizon. I had gone up there with my parents last summer to see the ancient cliff dwellings that were built centuries ago along the canyon rims that cut through that area. It was part of Mesa Verde National Park. We saw some wild horses while we were there, but the park ranger told us that there were no horses in North America when the cliff dwellings were being built and lived in. I couldn't imagine life here without horses.

Up ahead were the snow-capped peaks of the La Plata Mountains. We would be turning off the road long before we reached the La Platas.

"Xender," I shouted, trying to make myself heard over the mooing and the footsteps of the cattle, "if we were going to ride all the way to the La Platas, how long do you think it would take us?"

"With or without the cows?" he asked.

"Well, with them, I guess," I said as I pictured covered wagons, oxen, cattle, men with long rifles, and women in long skirts and bonnets.

He thought for a few minutes. Finally, he said, "Most of three days, I suppose."

"Really?"

"Well, yeah. It took us less than twenty minutes to ride in a truck over to where we started this morning, but it's going to take us most of the day to drive the cattle to the cattle pens just past Grandpa's, which is where we're going to put them up for the night. So, yeah, I think we could get there in three days."

"Wow! Can you imagine driving cattle all the way across the Oregon Trail like the early settlers did? No wonder it took so long."

"They didn't have roads like we do either, so they would be traveling even slower," he pointed out. "But I think it'd be cool to do that—Spend every day, all day in the saddle!"

"Yeah, me too!"

Xender laughed. "*You* wouldn't be riding. You'd be walking alongside the wagons with the women, wearing a dress and a big ol' sunbonnet."

"I would not!" I objected.

Our argument was interrupted when we heard Violet yelling at us. I couldn't understand what she was saying, but Xender did. Pointing toward Violet who, I now realized, was blocking a dirt road off to the right, Xender said, "It's your turn."

"Finally!" I urged Rowdy into a lope and threaded my way through the cattle, along the shoulder of the road, till I got to where Violet was waiting.

She turned and rode away just as I got there. I positioned Rowdy in the middle of the side road and loosened the reins, counting on him to know what to do, which, of course, he did. If a cow so much as *looked* toward the turn-off, he would flatten his ears and swing his head in her direction. A few times, he had to take a small step or two, but with just a little body language, he was able to keep all the cows on the highway where they were supposed to be.

After the herd passed by, I dropped in behind.

"Xender," I asked, "why do you think the Charolais cattle keep trying to take side roads? They wanted to turn off back at that last gate again."

"Probably 'cause it's their first year on the cattle drive, so they don't know where they're going or how nice it is up there. Mrs. Carlton just bought them a few weeks ago. She told me once that she showed Charolais cattle in 4-H when she was a kid and really liked them. Mr. Carlton finally told her that if they were as good as she kept bragging, they ought to add a few of them to the herd. So she did."

Just then, I noticed the entrance to an old ranch that had been converted into a subdivision.

"Xender," I asked, pointing. "Why isn't anyone blocking that?"

"Cattle guard," he said.

"Uh, what?"

"There's a cattle guard there already. We don't need to worry about it."

I didn't see anybody up there, but he didn't seem worried, so I stayed at the back of the herd and kept watching. When we got up to the entryway, I realized that a cattle guard was an "it," not a "who." It was made of a series of heavy-duty metal pipes, three or four inches apart, that stretched across the dirt lane between the gate posts. It covered an area that was probably six feet wide and fifteen feet long. Under the pipes, it was hollow. Any animal trying to walk through it would step into the spaces between the pipes and get stuck. But a car or truck could easily drive across it. The cows all kept their distance from it.

The next stretch of road went across the top of the dam that held back Narraguinnep Reservoir. There were guardrails on both sides of the road, so our herd was crowded together, now taking up both lanes. Any driver brave enough to drive through them had to go super slow, while the cattle separated and walked around their vehicle.

I guess that's why I noticed one particular driver in a battered old truck. It took him so long to drive through the herd that I had time to think about where I'd seen him before. It was Mr. Hillson, the embezzler.

He was really taking his time; he seemed more interested in looking at the cattle than driving through the herd. After what seemed like forever, he made it through and went on his way. I took a deep breath and felt myself start to relax. He was creepy, and I was glad to have him out of my sight.

Once past the reservoir, the road went through an area of pinyon pine and juniper trees, with a fence forty feet back on each side of the highway. It was fun looking back into the trees. I spotted some mule deer bedded down in the shadows, their big ears flipping at flies as they dozed. Looking at them made me yawn.

Reminding myself that I needed to stay alert, I decided to pull off my sweatshirt and tie it onto the back of the saddle. And while I was at it, I pulled out my water bottle. The water tasted cool and good.

I was twisted around in the saddle, putting the bottle away when I heard Xender shouting.

Chapter 8
Meghan Becomes a Tourist Attraction

I looked where Xender was pointing. Some of the cows had found a hole in the fence on his side of the road. Signaling Rowdy with my legs and reins, we quickly caught up with Xender and followed him through the gap in the fence. Fortunately the trees were not very thick and it was easy to see where the escapees had gone.

I didn't let Rowdy completely take over as I had been doing. I knew from experience that when a horse goes past trees, he only cares that there's enough room for him to make it through. It doesn't occur to him that your head and upper body stick up higher than he does, or that your knees stick further out to the side. If there's room for him, he goes. So I guided him in a more round-about path than he wanted to take. But eventually, Xender and I both got ahead of the cattle and turned them back toward where they had come through the fence. They weren't very cooperative though, since we were having to drive them the opposite direction from the rest of the herd. The cows kept trying to turn and go past us, which Rowdy wasn't going to allow. I was actually glad I had my helmet on as we smashed through some tree branches.

We finally got the cattle back to the broken section of fence and put them through—all except for one little calf, who couldn't quite work it out. He mooed and bawled, wanting to go with his momma, but no matter how much we tried, we couldn't get him to find the gap through the fence. Finally we jumped off our horses. Xender got on one side of the calf, and I got on the other. Rowdy and Xender's horse, Scout, blocked his escape from behind as we guided and shoved him forward and out through the fence. As soon as he was free, he raced after his mother, who was trotting up the road, trying to catch up with the herd. We quickly hopped back up on our horses and loped along behind.

Mr. Searle gave us a big grin and a "Well done!" as we passed his truck and trailer.

A few minutes later, we heard a squeal of brakes behind us as a car came over the hill and had to stop quickly to keep from rear-ending Mr. Searle's trailer. The driver pulled out around him and started trying to navigate her way through the herd.

"Guess she's in a hurry," Xender observed drily.

I think Xender must have been right because the driver started honking her horn.

"This is gonna be good! I love it when this happens," Xender said. "Watch!"

Instead of moving away, the cows abruptly turned and started toward her, completely surrounding her car. She finally had to brake the car to a stop. In apparent frustration, she continued honking, but the more she honked, the more tightly the cattle packed around her.

I looked over at Xender, wanting to ask what it was all about, but he was laughing so hard I could never have understood his answer, so I stayed quiet and kept watching.

Ben rode toward her and started slashing his hand in front of his throat, as if to say, 'Knock it off.' She apparently got the message because she finally stopped honking. The cows gradually lost interest and resumed their march. At long last, there was enough room for her to continue, slowly, through the herd.

Xender finally quieted down, and I was able to ask, "Why did the cows do that?"

That was enough to send him into peals of laughter once more. Between guffaws, he explained: "During the winter, when the ranchers have to haul hay into the fields for the cattle, they honk their horns to let the cows know it's feeding time. When that woman started honking, the cows figured she was ringing the dinner bell so they went to see what she had for them."

The rest of the morning passed without any major drama—or comedy. The cows in the back, where we were riding, seemed less and less interested in finding any side routes. They could see the rest of the herd strung out up ahead and were mostly content to follow along. Every so often, we had to rescue a calf who found his way through a bad spot in the fence, but that was about the extent of our problems.

Ben rode back to see us later in the morning. "I'll ride drag for a while," he said. "You two get up there in front of the herd and station your horses at the entrance to the *Canyon of the Ancients Museum*. I expect you'll have some fun there. But most important, I trust you two to keep any cows from wandering up to the museum parking lot."

Xender and I turned our mounts onto the dirt shoulder and took off at a lope, arriving at the entryway just ahead of the leading edge of the herd. We positioned our horses, one on the exit lane, one on the entrance.

I began intently watching the cows for any who even looked in my direction, ready to head them off if necessary. As a result, I didn't notice a car attempting to exit the museum, until it was squeezing past me, trying to get out onto the road with the cows. The people in the car were locals; I recognized one of the girls from school, so seeing a cattle drive didn't faze them a bit. But they made me realize that, along with watching for cows, we were going to have to keep an eye out for cars entering and leaving the museum too.

The next time a car came up behind me, I heard it and turned to wave them around me. But the car, which had a New York license plate, came to a stop, and all of its occupants tumbled out, excitedly pointing and shouting.

"Look at all those cows!"

"Are you a cowboy, er, girl?"

"Can I pet your horse?"

I wasn't sure how to answer, when suddenly Xender's voice cut in. "Stay back from the horses, please. They're working! And if they have to go after the cows all of a sudden, you'll get stepped on."

That stopped the tourists a few feet back from us.

"Can we take your picture?"

"Uh, sure," I said.

I heard cameras clicking, but I also heard another car coming down the exit lane. I turned to try to direct them around us, but the New Yorkers took over, stopping the car and telling the occupants that they could not pet the horses, but they could take all the pictures they wanted.

Before long we had such a huge crowd behind us that no cow in her right mind would have tried to approach the entryway. Just when I thought it couldn't get any crazier, a busload of Japanese tourists got out. The New Yorkers had no luck communicating with them. Some of them walked right into the road to get close-ups of the cows. They even tried to pet the calves. Another group surrounded me, their cameras clicking all around. As quickly as they had appeared, they retreated back onto their bus.

The New Yorkers just grinned at us, with their palms up in the air, as if to say, "We tried." Then one of them asked, "Now, can we pet your horse, since the cows are past?"

"Um, sure," I said. "But I have to catch up, so I can't stay long."

A few pats and camera clicks later, and we were back on duty, riding drag.

The herd had gradually stretched out over a longer distance. The cows with older calves were mostly toward the front with the younger ones lagging behind.

Ben rode back to see us. "I need you two to ride up toward the front of the herd and take over for Casey and Cody. Tell them I need 'em back here. And check in with Mr. Carlton. He'll tell you what to do when you get to the next turn or two."

Loping up to the front, we delivered our messages and took the lead. Before long, we came to a curve where the main part of the road went right, while a smaller dirt road branched off to the left, down toward McPhee Reservoir, which was even bigger than the last reservoir we had ridden past.

"The cows are probably going to want to turn here and go down to the water," Mr. Carlton warned us. "We're going to have our work cut out for us till we get the first part of the herd past this turn and headed up the hill."

The next few minutes were a lot of fun! Our horses were amazing, jumping back and forth, turning back any of the cows that tried to split from the herd, and chasing them away from the dirt road. Rowdy was totally awesome, and I was having the best time ever!

Soon the first part of the herd was around the bend and heading up the hill. The rest of the cows followed along placidly, no longer challenging us.

Less than a mile on, we came to another T in the road and made the turn toward Dolores. Once again, we were on a main highway. But with the herd stretched out as it was, there was at least one clear lane for the traffic to get past us.

I recognized one of the cars coming toward us. It was Dad's car. He was driving and waving, while Mom was hanging out the passenger side, snapping pictures on her phone. "We have to run some errands in town, honey," Mom yelled as they drove past. "We'll be home in a few hours."

As we moved the herd down the long hill into town, I wondered out loud, "Are we really going to drive them straight up the main street?"

"Yep, right up the middle of Railroad Avenue," Xender said. "And except for one spot, it should go pretty smoothly."

"Let me guess: the Dolores Market?"

"That's the spot. Right before the Market, the cattle will want to turn and head down the side road to the river. I'll block the road, if you can protect the flowers. Then we also have to make sure they don't head for the park beside the town hall."

"Sure!" I could picture what he meant. There was a raised flower garden in front of the market. The cows were sure to think that was a feed trough, just for them. And I was sure that the town hall lawn would look pretty tempting too.

Coming into town, one of the first buildings we passed was the Chamber of Commerce office. Someone ran outside with a camera and started snapping pictures.

A few blocks later we got out in front of the cattle and were able to keep them from turning to the river or eating the flowers. Several cows wandered over toward the town hall park, but some high school boys carrying skateboards chased them back toward the road.

It was more work, but it was also a lot of fun going through town, as people came out of their businesses to wave as we went past. Many of the buildings were old, and some had an old-fashioned boardwalk in front. If I used my imagination—and could ignore the cars—it kind of felt like the Old West.

Unfortunately, I was about to find out that I couldn't ignore the cars.

Chapter 9
A Close Call

The herd cleared the far edge of town at last, and I knew we were on the final stretch for today. There were some cattle pens just beyond Ben's place where we were going to keep them overnight so they could eat, drink, and rest in preparation for tomorrow's drive.

"Do you want to lead, or do you want to drop back a little and help keep the cattle over on this side of the road?" Xender called.

"I'll go back," I shouted, as I turned Rowdy and walked down the centerline of the highway, crowding cows and calves over toward the shoulder. They moved over agreeably.

Farther back, I could see Ben keeping the back part of the herd pushed over to the side, too, so I turned around to face the front of the herd. Rowdy and I walked along in the middle of one lane, leaving the other lane clear for traffic.

As we plodded along, I watched the cattle, mildly surprised at how much manure the cows were still pumping out. It seemed to me that the entire highway must be covered with it from here all the way back to where we had started this morning.

Hearing the noise of an engine coming up behind us, I glanced back to make sure the cattle were off to the side. A few of the cows were walking close to the centerline, but the other lane was completely clear, leaving plenty of room for the car.

I was totally caught off guard when the driver suddenly laid on the horn, especially since it didn't sound like a car horn, but more like a loud train whistle. The sudden, unfamiliar noise startled the cows and calves behind me, and they bolted forward in panic, crashing into Rowdy's hind legs. He stumbled sideways, hit a patch of slick, wet manure, and fell.

As he went down, I managed to pull my foot out of the stirrup to land straddling him. I stepped off just as the car careened past, barely missing us. Poor old Rowdy clambered back to his feet and stood, spraddle-legged and unsteady. Blood was already seeping from the scrapes and cuts where his legs had road-rashed against the highway.

I heard Ben's voice shouting, "Meghan, are you okay?!"

"Rowdy's hurt!" I cried. Then, realizing I hadn't answered his question, I added, "I'm fine." No point in mentioning that my heart was pounding about a thousand miles an hour, and I was nearly choking on anger at the driver.

Ben was loping down the far shoulder of the road. Within a minute he was off his horse and beside me, running his hands down Rowdy's legs. "Lead him a few steps," he ordered as he straightened up.

I whispered, "Come on, ol' buddy," and eased forward. Rowdy hobbled valiantly along behind me as I struggled to hold back my tears.

"Well, it's not great," Ben said, shaking his head. "But it's a long ways from his heart, and he should heal up just fine in a few weeks."

"What should I do?" I asked, willing myself not to cry.

Ben looked at me sharply. "Are you sure you're okay?"

I nodded.

"Okay then. Here's what I need you to do. Walk him to the ranch. It's only another quarter of a mile up the road. Unsaddle him and let him have a drink of water. Then drag the hose out and run water on his legs. Don't splash it directly on the cuts though. Aim the hose above the cuts and let the water run down over 'em. Savvy?"

"Yes sir. I can do that."

"Hose him for at least twenty minutes. As soon as we get these cattle penned up, I'll get straight back to the ranch. I've got some medication that should help him. Meanwhile, you'll need to keep him where his legs can dry off after you're done hosin' him. And don't let him roll 'cause that'll just get his legs dirty again."

The herd had continued to move past us while we talked, so by now we were just about in the middle.

"I need to get up ahead and help Xender," Ben said as he swung back into his saddle. "You sure you're okay?"

"Just worried about Rowdy," I said, wiping away a tear that had finally managed to leak out. "I'll take good care of him, Ben. You go on."

As soon as Ben was gone, I eased Rowdy forward. Watching him limp along beside me, I quit trying to stop them, and those tears ran down my cheeks like a river. Rowdy was such a wonderful horse. He didn't deserve this. I kept replaying the scene over and over in my mind. What could I have done to prevent his getting hurt? The more I thought about it, the more my stomach knotted up.

By the time we got to Ben's ranch I was sure the wreck had been my fault. Ben had once described someone as "lower than a snake's belly." I hadn't really understood what he meant by that. Until today. But that was exactly how I felt.

Slowly, I led Rowdy down the lane, past my house, and all the way back to the barn, where I tied him to the hitching rack. Then I dragged the saddle off his back and lugged it to the tack room.

Returning with a bucket, I unrolled the hose and filled the pail with clean, fresh water. While Rowdy drank, I started running the hose on his legs above the cuts, as Ben had told me. The cuts were pretty yucky to look at, so I glanced away for a second. That's when I realized I was causing another problem. If I kept hosing him off for twenty minutes at the hitching rack, we were going to have a giant mudhole. Untying Rowdy, I led him away from it and dragged the hose to a grassy patch where the water wouldn't make such a big mess. Rowdy approved of this change in location and went straight to munching the grass.

Twenty minutes is a long, long, long time when it's spent thinking about what you could have done better to keep from getting your best friend hurt. When the time was finally up, my head was pounding like a drum. I coiled the hose back up and grabbed a curry comb and brush. While Rowdy continued to graze, I gave him a thorough grooming, currying his itchy spots where the saddle had been, as well as across his chest and between his front legs where he had been sweating.

At last, I heard Ben's truck and trailer coming up the lane.

"You two kids get my horse taken care of along with yours," he called back over his shoulder to Xender and Violet as he stepped out of the truck.

He walked straight toward Rowdy and me.

I will not cry. I will not cry. I will not cry, I kept telling myself. Out loud I said, "I'm so sorry, Ben. If I had been more careful, Rowdy wouldn't have gotten hurt."

Ben stopped in his tracks and looked at me. Then his eyes shifted to Rowdy. "What do you mean? Has somethin' else happened?"

"No," I said, feeling a little confused.

"Well then, you don't owe anyone an apology," he stated bluntly. "You aren't to blame for the actions of some stupid, self-important show-off."

"But if I had been paying more attention, I would have seen it coming and could've gotten Rowdy out of the way."

"I doubt it, Meghan. I don't think any of us could have anticipated the kind of noisemaker that knothead was using for a horn. I'm just glad Rowdy didn't break his leg. Or yours. You did well gettin' yer foot out of the stirrup when he was falling." He hesitated, chuckling. "And I'm real glad about that 'cause I would *not* have enjoyed explaining to yer parents that their baby girl had broken her leg on her first cattle drive."

I giggled in agreement.

"It's muddy over here. Meghan made a mess with the hose!" Violet complained.

"Quit yer bellyachin'," Ben responded. "All she did was wet down the dust a little. Looks to me like she was smart enough to hose his legs off on the grass." Ben grinned at me, then turned back to Violet. "And don't you think you're goin' to dump all the work on yer brother this time. You go help him with my horse, young lady."

A Close Call

Ben walked past Violet into the barn, returning a few minutes later with his equine first aid kit. While I held Rowdy's lead rope, Ben gently applied medication to the injuries. "He should be good as new in a few weeks."

My heart sank. I mean, I was thrilled that Rowdy would be okay. But there were two more days of driving cattle, and I was suddenly afoot.

Cowgirls Don't Quit

Chapter 10
A Horse of a Different Color

"You let me do the talkin'," Ben said quietly as we walked toward my house, where Mom and Dad were carrying grocery sacks inside. I nodded. I had been grateful when he said he would walk me home 'cause I wasn't looking forward to explaining what had happened or the fact that I wouldn't be going tomorrow.

Mom saw us and called out, "How was it, Meghan?"

Uh oh. How was I supposed to let Ben do the talking when Mom was asking me a direct question? I glanced up at Ben.

"Answer her. But make it short," he whispered.

"It was great!" I said with as much enthusiasm as I could muster. But Mom had noticed the hesitation. She had that look of suspicion she gets when she knows I'm trying to hide something.

Ben jumped right in. "You can be real proud of this young lady. She did a fine job today and proved herself to be not just a rider but a real hand. She was a big help with the cattle, and she also treated her horse right. That means a lot to me."

Mom and Dad both smiled and hugged me. Then Mom looked Ben right in the eye. "But what?"

"Well," he drawled, "just before we got back to the ranch, ol' Rowdy hit a slick spot on the highway and fell," Ben said as casually as possible.

Mom's eyes got big. She grabbed me by the shoulders and looked me up and down. "Are you all right?"

"I'm fine, Mom! Not a scratch." I spun around slowly to show her I wasn't hiding anything.

"So why are you trying not to cry?"

How could she always tell? I answered miserably, "Because Rowdy's hurt."

Ben clarified, "He's not hurt bad. Just some cuts and scrapes. But it was enough that he's not going to be able to go tomorrow. That's why I wanted to talk with you. I've got another horse that Meghan can ride. After watching her with Rowdy today, I have no doubt that she will get along jes' fine with this horse."

I could hardly believe my ears! I looked back and forth from Ben to my parents, waiting for someone to say something.

Realizing that my parents weren't looking entirely convinced, Ben resumed, "Meghan truly was a big help to us today. We would all be mighty pleased if she could go along tomorrow. And she learned a lot. Riding a different horse will be good experience for her, and she'll learn even more."

"Please, Mom? Dad?" I pleaded.

My parents exchanged looks. Finally, I saw a slight nod from both of them, and I knew they were about to agree. "Okay. If you're sure, Ben."

Walking over to the ranch in the early morning moonlight, I wondered which horse I was going to get to ride today. I had started to text Xender after dinner to see if he knew. But when the alarm went off in the morning, my phone was lying on my bed next to me with a half-written, unsent text message. I guess I had been tireder than I thought.

Ben already had his big training horse tied to the hitching rack and was carrying a halter with him as he walked away from the colt. He saw me coming and said, "Get him brushed off, then bring yer saddle out. I'll throw it up on his back fer ya." He chuckled, then added, "He's a mite taller than you're used to."

I stopped and stared. Had I understood correctly? Was I really going to ride Freckles?

"Well, don't jes' stand there. Get a brush and get busy," Ben commanded as he walked away.

I did as he told me, but it was weird trying to curry a horse's back when his back was over my head. I worked really hard, both currying and brushing, especially those places I couldn't see. By the time Ben got back with another horse, I was starting to clean his feet.

"Where are Xender and Violet?" I asked.

"Xender is out in the field trying to catch his horse. Ol' Scout took a notion that he didn't want to get caught this mornin'." Ben chuckled. Then, with less amusement in his voice, he added, "And Violet is still in the house gettin' all beautified. How 'bout if you grab a bucket of grain and bring Rowdy in so I can look at his legs. Maybe you can help Xender whilst yer at it."

I got the grain and carried it out to the pasture, shaking it. Rowdy hobbled up to me, and I let him have a bite of it while I rubbed him on the neck. "I'm sorry you can't come with us today, Rowdy. I hope you don't mind too much getting left behind, but you have to stay here and start feeling better."

While I was talking to Rowdy, Scout walked up to see what I had in the bucket, and I managed to slip my rope over his neck. Once Xender caught up to me, he put his own halter on Scout and mumbled, "Thank you." He sounded embarrassed that he couldn't catch his own horse.

I put a halter on Rowdy and led him over to the hitching rack. "Ben, his legs are really swollen."

"Yeah, I figured they'd be pretty puffy by this morning. That's Mother Nature's way." Ben knelt down and treated the cuts again. "Now put him back out in the field so he can enjoy his day off." As I walked back toward the gate, Ben called, "Meghan."

"Yes sir?"

"Don't you go bein' nice and catchin' Violet's horse. She's on her own this mornin'."

I put Rowdy back into the field, pulled off his halter, and gave him one more hug. Then I turned and ran back to the barn to help saddle Freckles.

"Can you get yer foot up to that stirrup and climb up on top of him?" Ben asked.

"I think so," I grunted, as I tried to mount the big colt. He was a good five inches taller than Rowdy, and it took some serious stretching, but I finally got it done. Once I was on top, I felt as if I was way more than five inches higher off the ground. Wow, he was big!

"I hope you've got some tissues in yer pockets, in case you get nose bleeds from the altitude," Ben joked. Then he started handing out the serious advice. "This colt is real quiet and sensible, but he's still a colt, so you're going to have to be a little more aware of what's going on around you. Aware. Not scared. If you get scared of something, yer horse will sense that fear and get scared right along with you. Savvy?"

I nodded. That was one of the first things Ben had taught me, and he had reminded me at least once a week since then.

"Just relax, and ride him like you would Rowdy. He doesn't have as much experience working cattle as Rowdy does, but he's naturally cowy. He likes bossin' 'em around. He might not always see what needs to be done, the way Rowdy does, so you may have to encourage him or help him get to the right place once in a while. But after you do, just give him his head and let him work. And holler anytime you've got concerns."

As Ben mounted one of his other training horses, Violet finally showed up. Ben turned toward her and said, with no detectable hint of sarcasm or reproach, "Well, don't you look positively beautiful this morning, Violet."

Violet looked at him suspiciously.

"You go ahead and get your horse caught, brush him off, saddle him, and catch up with us as quick as you can. If you're there before we have the herd out onto the highway, you can pick yer spot. Otherwise, I'll be telling you what section of the herd you'll be workin'. Oh," he added in his don't-even-think-about-arguing tone of voice, "remember to wear your helmet, or you will find yerself afoot today."

"See you soon," added Xender sarcastically, not quite laughing at his sister.

We turned and started out the lane. I looked at Xender questioningly. He explained, "Grandpa told Violet that she was going to have to get her horse ready herself today if she planned to go with us. He knows she *really* wants to go this time, 'cause the Carlton's son, Jace, got home from college last night, and he's going to be helping today." Xender's voice went high and squeaky in a less-than-flattering imitation of his sister. "Violet thinks he's 'just the handsomest thing ever to put on a pair of Wrangler jeans.'"

The almost full moon lit our way, along with the promise of sunrise that glowed in the eastern sky. As we rode out the lane toward the highway, Ben handed each of us a vest made of reflective material. "Put that on," he told me.

Freckles didn't seem at all concerned as I squirmed into the vest. He really did seem like a big sweetie. Even so, not gonna lie, I was still a little weirded out by the bigness of him. I felt so high above the ground, and his neck was so long that his head seemed too far away. Then there was his walk. He took huge steps with those long, gangly legs of his. He was definitely going to take some getting used to.

It wasn't much more than a ten-minute ride to where the cattle were penned up, but that was enough for me to start getting comfortable on Freckles. He responded to my legs and my reins even more lightly than Rowdy did. That was pretty cool.

When we arrived at the cattle pens, Mr. Searle said he'd be leading today, because Mrs. Carlton was running a little late. He pulled his rig onto the highway and shouted, "Move 'em out." With that, Ben opened the gate while Casey and Cody, who were already in with the cows, began yipping and hollering, urging the cows and calves through the gate.

Ben, Xender, and I kept the cattle from turning in the wrong direction, while Mr. Carlton and a boy I didn't recognize, but figured must've been Jace, moved forward with the front of the herd. Seeing Jace made me think about Violet, and I looked over my shoulder to see if she was coming up the road. I didn't see her, but I did see the headlights of a truck and trailer approaching.

Mrs. Carlton stopped Ben's truck behind us. Jumping out she shouted cheerily, "Thanks for leaving the keys in the truck for me, Ben!"

We were surprised when Violet stepped out the passenger side, walked back, and unloaded her horse from the trailer.

"I guess Violet was running a little late this morning too," Mrs. Carlton said.

As Violet led her horse past Mrs. Carlton she said sweetly, and loud enough for her Grandpa to hear, "Thank you very much for the lift."

Mrs. Carlton smiled and winked. "You're welcome, Violet. We girls have to stick together."

To her grandpa, Violet said, "It doesn't look as if the whole herd is out of the pen yet, so I think I will choose to work up at the front today." She mounted up, kicked her horse, and loped up the shoulder of the road to where Jace was riding.

Ben just shook his head.

Chapter 11
Justice

While we waited for the rest of the herd to come out onto the road, Mrs. Carlton walked over to Ben and me. "I saw what happened yesterday, so I wrote down the license number and a description of the car that honked and spooked the cattle into poor ol' Rowdy. Then I called my brother." Turning to me, she paused for effect and said, "He's the deputy sheriff up in Rico."

Ben started smiling as if he already knew the answer to the question he was about to ask: "And was your brother on duty yesterday?"

"As a matter of fact, he was. And when that car pulled into town, would you believe it was going nearly fifteen miles per hour over the speed limit? My brother, of course, was obliged to stop the driver and ticket him. Then he did a quick check to make sure the car's lights, the turn signals, and the *horn* were all working properly, which they were. He mentioned to the driver that a horn like that was loud enough to scare a herd of cattle. I'm told the driver got kind of a funny look on his face when he said that."

"I'll bet he did," said Ben.

"After writing the speeding ticket, he sent the driver on his way. Well, apparently the driver was trying to make up for lost time as he left Rico. You know that area where it stays 45 miles an hour for a while? Well he got a little overanxious and hit 55 way too soon and, as luck would have it, he got stopped for speeding *again* by one of my brother's co-workers. He ticketed the driver and then checked his lights and horns and mentioned to him that a horn like that would scare a herd of cattle. Rumor has it that the driver got a *really* funny look on his face that time."

Ben chuckled.

"Oh, it gets better," Mrs. Carlton continued gleefully. "You know that area between Ophir and Telluride where the speed limit drops to 25? Well this poor driver apparently didn't notice the sign, and an officer-friend of my brother's who works in that county, stopped him and ticketed him and checked his lights and horn. Before he could say a word about it, the driver asked, 'Officer, if I promise never to honk my horn near a herd of cattle again, is there any chance that I will be permitted to get to Grand Junction tonight?' The officer told him that he *might* be able to do that, but only if he also learned how to read speed limit signs."

"Three speeding tickets and the fines that go with them... I'd say that feller learned a lesson yesterday that he won't soon forget," Ben said. He tipped his hat to Mrs. Carlton. "I thank you, ma'am, and I would be most appreciative if you would pass along my gratitude to your brother and his friends."

Mrs. Carlton smiled. "I will be happy to do that," she promised, "but it will have to wait 'til later because we are about to run out of cell phone service." She turned and hurried back to the truck, taking up her position behind us as the last of the cattle came out of the pen.

Casey and Cody followed them onto the road, then crossed to the far shoulder and broke into a lope to move up to the middle of the herd.

"I'm gonna stay back here with you two for a while," Ben said. "This is the first time this filly has been on a drive, so I'd like to keep her back till she gets the idea."

The young mare appeared to be doing quite well. I wondered if the real reason he was sticking around was because he was worried about Freckles and me.

Out loud I asked, "How did Freckles get his name? He doesn't have any kind of spots on him that I can see."

"Many Quarter Horses, which is the kinda horse he is, are named for their parents or grandparents. His grandsire was Colonel Freckles, who was a well-known cuttin' horse."

"So is there more to his name than just 'Freckles'?"

"There most assuredly is. And since I just looked at a copy of his registration papers a few days ago, I should know what it is." Ben stopped talking and thought for a minute. "But, nope. I'm not rememberin' it."

"That's okay. I just wondered."

Ben shrugged. "I'm afraid I don't much care what a horse's name is. All I care is if the horse has a good mind, a willin' attitude, and nice way of movin'. And Freckles has got all that."

Just then part of the herd started to split off toward a grassy patch on the far side of the road. I urged Freckles forward, and we herded them back to the other side. A few minutes later a calf got stuck between some thick brush and the fence that ran along the road. Xender and I hurried over, jumped off our horses and rescued him. I lined Freckles up on the low side of the shoulder of the road and was able to mount back up from the high side without *too* much trouble.

Farther along, I saw two driveways that went through gaps in the fence. Cody was blocking one and Casey the other. Xender and I loped up to them and took over so they could move to the middle of the herd again.

Loping Freckles was amazing. On Rowdy, I'd had trouble keeping up with Xender and Scout when we loped. Now, with Freckles' long strides, I was in the lead.

Casey moved out of his spot as I approached, so I stopped Freckles where Casey had been and turned the big horse to watch the cows. Xender got there right after us and took over for Cody. Freckles watched the cows like a hawk. If a cow looked in his direction, he lowered his head, flattened his ears, and seemed able to tell her that challenging him would be a mistake. Only a few cows didn't get the message, but even then, it took only a few quick steps to head them off. He was different from Rowdy, but he was just as much fun!

Once the herd had passed, we fell in behind them again.

"Well," Ben drawled, "I think it's time to move up and show this filly some different scenery."

"Sure, Grandpa," Xender said.

"It's okay with me," I agreed.

Ben jogged the filly ahead. I smiled to myself. We must have passed the test. Ben no longer felt obligated to stay back and babysit us.

I pulled my cell phone out and took a look at the screen.

"What do you think you're doing?" asked Xender. "Didn't you hear what Mrs. Carlton said? There's pretty much no service up here."

"But why not?" I asked. "I mean it's not like this is a dirt road. This is the main road from the Four Corners up to Telluride."

"Doesn't matter," Xender said. "Look around."

I looked. On my right, I could see the Dolores River rushing along muddily as it carried the spring runoff down from the high mountain peaks. Beyond the narrow meadow where the river raged, the tree-covered mountains went up at a steep angle. On my left, just beyond the shoulder of the highway, more mountains.

"I guess I didn't realize how narrow and steep this valley is."

"Why are you so worried about your phone anyway? You're not going to turn into another Violet are you, checking your phone every three seconds?"

"No!" I objected. "It's just that Mom told me to call her around lunchtime to let her know how things are going. She's all worried."

"That's what moms do best," Xender said. "But there's nothing you can do to change the facts. You're not going to be calling."

"She is going to be *so* not happy with me," I moaned. But there was nothing I could do about it. I turned my phone off to save the battery and stuffed it back into my pocket.

Other than worrying that Mom was going to ground me for the rest of my life, it was a great day. With no phone and no way to know what time it was, I felt even more like a pioneer. Okay, except for all the cars, trucks, and RVs that crawled past us all day. When I got hungry, I pulled food out of my saddlebag, not caring if it was lunchtime or not, though I think it was, because Freckles' shadow was pretty much underneath him.

While I was eating my apple, I bit off chunks, leaned forward, and fed some of them to Freckles. He munched them happily. "Do you remember when you first arrived at Ben's last fall, Freckles? I tried to feed you apples then, but you spit them out as if you thought I was trying to poison you. Remember how Ben laughed at me and told me that young horses have to learn about special treats, and that if I wanted to teach you to like apples, I would have to be persistent and patient. It's a good thing our apple tree had a big crop last year 'cause it must've taken three weeks to get you to eat them. Now I think you like them as much as I do!"

We caught up with Xender about then. He had been defending a driveway on the right.

"Why do girls always have to talk to their horses?" he asked.

"Same reasons that you do, probably! And don't pretend that you don't talk to Scout, 'cause I've heard you."

"That's different," he said, but I noticed he didn't make any attempt to explain why.

On straight stretches of road, I could see to the front of the herd, where Violet was never more than three feet away from Jace, which always made me giggle.

"I'll bet Violet isn't talking to *her* horse," I said.

"Nope. She's too busy talking to Jace and flirting with him," Xender said, imitating Violet batting her eyes.

"If she looks like that when she does, I'm surprised Jace lets her anywhere near him."

"Yeah, well, I'm just glad she's up there, and we're at the other end of the herd so we don't have to listen to her."

Most of the time, because of all the turns in the road as it followed the Dolores River, we could only see as far as where Ben was riding, so we didn't have to look at Violet very often.

I still could hardly believe Ben was letting me ride as cool a horse as Freckles. Not that I didn't miss Rowdy, because he was great, too, but Freckles was so interested in everything. He watched the cows like he was supposed to, but he was super aware of other things going on around us as well. He would suddenly turn his head to look up into the woods on the mountain beside us, and when I looked in the same direction, I often saw elk or deer watching us pass by. Once, he spotted a coyote trotting across a meadow on the other side of the river. And we saw lots of red tailed hawks.

The day went by way too fast, even without knowing the time, and we arrived at the next stopping point long before I wanted to. We penned the cattle into the corrals at a ranch just off the highway and loaded our horses into the trailers for the drive back down the canyon.

The whole way home, I worried how my parents were going to react about my not calling them. I got out my phone and turned it on, planning to call as soon as we were in cell phone range again.

Justice

As we got close to Dolores, I was startled when my phone buzzed at me. I looked and saw there was a voicemail from Mom. Actually, I was kind of surprised that there weren't at least a hundred voicemails from her. I pushed the button to listen, mentally bracing myself for the tongue-lashing I knew was coming. To my complete surprise, I heard her cheery voice saying, "I just realized you probably won't be able to call me today. We'll see you when you get home."

Really? I worried all day for nothing?

"Xender," I asked while we were unloading the horses, "have you ever noticed that parents never react the way you think they're going to?"

"Yours, too?" he responded. "I thought mine were the only ones. Sometimes I do stuff that I think they're going to be mad about, and they actually keep their cool."

"Yeah," I agreed. "Then you do something harmless and they totally come unglued about it. Why is that?"

"I don't know."

"I think parents should come with an instruction manual," I told him.

"Or warning labels."

Cowgirls Don't Quit

Chapter 12
Muffled Voices

The next morning, we didn't have to be ready to go quite as early as usual. Ben had told us that the day's drive would cover the shortest distance. Besides, he wanted to delay a little so that we would have full daylight when we turned off the highway and started up the mountain. By the time we got the cattle out of their pen, the morning sun was already well above the horizon.

It felt good to be back on Freckles, following along behind the cows and their calves. I still loved Rowdy, but riding a big horse was fun.

The first couple of miles went fast, and I was surprised how soon it was time to turn off the highway and head up the trail to the top of Taylor Mesa. The cows were really frisky. It was as if they knew they were getting close to their summer range. They seemed as happy as my classmates and me getting out of school a week and a half ago. Wow. Was that all it had been? This had already been my most fun summer ever, and it had just started!

Ben rode back to join us. "I'm going to ride with you two today. We won't have a truck and trailer behind us to help once we turn up the trail into the mountains. The three of us are going to have to make sure we don't lose any stragglers or have any of 'em turn the wrong way before they get to the gates."

"Yes sir!" Xender and I answered in unison.

"The cows know where they're going, and they're anxious to get up there. Anxious enough that they may not realize if a calf has gotten left behind. Once one of 'em does remember, she may come charging back through the rest of the herd to find her baby. If you end up working further along in the herd today and you see a cow charging toward the back of the herd, don't try to stop her. Savvy?"

"Yes sir!"

When the cows ahead of us turned and started up the trail, I thought it looked as if the whole herd was being swallowed up by the tree-covered mountains. Finally, we, too, reached the turn and followed behind them into the dark trees. The trail was rough, with rocks and tree limbs that the horses and cattle had to step over or go around. No wonder Ben wanted it to be full daylight before we got to that point.

We hadn't gone very far when we came to a meadow where the cows were bunched up. Instead of moving forward, the mommas were grazing, and most of the calves were nursing. On the uphill side of the herd, I could see that Cody, Casey, and Jace were off their horses, trying to open a gate that went through a wire fence.

"It's sure nice having those boys with us," Ben commented. "That's a miserable excuse for a gate, and I'm happy to have them deal with it."

After a moment's hesitation, Xender asked, "Um, who's going to close it?"

"No one. In fact, I'm kinda surprised it was shut. We haven't closed it in years," Ben said, looking around as he did. He seemed puzzled. Finally he continued, "The gate is narrow, so even when they get it open, it's gonna take awhile for the herd to get on through it. For now, we may as well just relax and enjoy the view."

After all the travel over the past couple of days, it was actually nice standing still, watching the cattle, seeing the new green leaves on the aspen trees at the far end of the meadow, smelling the pine trees, listening to the birds, and feeling an occasional soft breeze, all while sitting on top of a really cool horse.

"Finally," Xender said. I looked up to see that the boys had gotten the gate open, and the first of the cows were resuming their trek up the mountain trail.

"Once the cattle get through, we'll follow along behind 'em. It's gonna be a different kind of ride than you're used to, Meghan, 'cause it's gonna start gettin' steep. When it does, stand up off yer horse's back and lean forward to make it easier on him," Ben advised. "And don't be shy about grabbin' the saddle horn."

Most of the cows headed willingly through the gate, but there were a few stragglers who were more interested in grazing in the meadow than going with the herd, so we had to spend a few minutes rounding them up and pushing them through. One of the Charolais cows and her calf didn't want to leave the far end of the meadow, and we really had to work to get them to rejoin the herd.

"Why's she being so stubborn?" I asked

"This is her first year up the trail," Xender reminded me. "She doesn't know yet that the good pasture is up on top."

Ben was waiting for us at the gate as we got the Charolais and her calf pushed through. "We're gonna be headin' through some rough country for the next twenty minutes or so. Mind what I said about standin' up and hangin' on."

Apparently Ben's idea of rough country meant mud holes to slog through, huge boulders to ride around, and more fallen trees to jump, all while ascending an amazingly steep trail. As we got higher on the mountain, we also had patches of snow to contend with. Lucky for me, Freckles didn't want to get left behind by the other horses. He looked pretty hard at some of the obstacles, but he was determined to keep up, and he managed to get over, around, or through every challenge. He was careful where he put his feet, too, never slipping or scrambling, as I saw Ben's filly do several times. *That* would have been terrifying. And it was already scary enough. All I could do was hang on and (mostly) enjoy the ride!

We slowed down at last, and I saw that the herd was once again gathered in a huge bunch just ahead of us. Beyond them, I could see another fence. The boys had already gotten the gate open, and the herd was filing through a few cows and calves at a time. The ones on this side of the fence were milling around, trying to mother up, with cows and calves mooing and bawling to one another.

Suddenly, one of the cows bolted straight toward us.

"Git out of her way!" shouted Ben. We quickly moved our horses off the trail. The cow swept past us and back down the way we had come. "Her calf must've got lost down below somewhere," Ben observed. "I'm sorry I didn't see it."

"Oh no! Poor thing," I worried. "How will she find her baby again?"

"Mother Nature has that all worked out. She'll jes' go back to where she last nursed the calf. Her baby will meet her there. Then they'll mosey back up the trail to find the herd."

There was nothing for us to do now but wait for the cows to sort themselves out and get through the gap in the next fence.

Xender shouted above the noise of the herd, "Well, what did you think of the trail?"

"It was wild!" I shouted back.

Ben commented, "Yeah. A little more deadfall than usual across the trail this year. I looked back a couple of times and was plumb happy to see you were still on top of that horse."

I felt a big smile spreading across my face. "That was the most fun ever!"

Before the last of the herd was through the fence, the runaway cow and her missing calf had come trotting back up the trail and rejoined us. We rode through the gate, and I saw that we were up on top of the mesa. Instead of being steep, the land was, well, not exactly flat, but sort of rolling, with large meadows surrounded by huge forests of aspen and pine. The herd had scattered, and I saw that the riders were making no attempt to keep them from doing so.

This was it, I realized sadly, the end of the cattle drive. Why did the fun stuff like this always have to fly by so fast?

"There's a dirt tank up yonder," Ben pointed and urged his horse in that direction. The rest of the riders followed along, so I turned Freckles to go too, wondering what a dirt tank might be. Shortly we came to a pond, where we let the horses all drink their fill. Freckles marched right into the water like a seasoned horse. I patted him on the neck.

"Why is it called a dirt tank?" I asked.

"What else would you call it?" Xender answered. "It's like a stock tank at home, but it's in the dirt." Xender shook his head as if it was the most obvious thing ever.

I'd have called it a pond, I thought to myself, but I didn't say it out loud. Cowboys had their own names for things, and Xender always got insulted if I thought the names were weird.

"Is this where the cattle will come for water all summer?" I asked.

"Oh no. There are other dirt tanks and springs scattered across the mesa," Xender said. "This area goes on for miles. You won't believe how big it is when we come up to gather the cows next fall."

I smiled. Next fall was going to be fun!

While the horses drank, we all pulled out our lunches for a quick picnic. While I ate, I watched the cows and their calves. I spotted the Charolais cow that we had had trouble getting through the lower gate. She was grazing on some of the new spring grass, her calf stretched out in the sun beside her, resting from the long climb.

It was beautiful here. Peaceful, too.

So, why was something bothering me? I was remembering Ben's surprise at the closed gate and trying to figure it out, when Violet rode over to me. "C'mon, Meghan. The ladies' room is over this way." As I followed her, I noticed that the guys were all heading for a clump of trees on the far side of the meadow.

Once we were into the woods, Violet jumped off her horse, handed me the reins, and ordered, "Wait here."

A few minutes later she came back, tucking in her shirt. "Your turn," she said, as she took her horse back. I dismounted and handed Freckles' reins to her. "And don't take all day," she shouted as I walked off to find a private bush.

Just as I was finishing up, I was startled by muffled voices in the distance. They seemed to be coming from down below, over the edge of the mountain. I quickly pulled up my jeans, looking around in embarrassment while I got them zipped and snapped. I couldn't see anyone. The sounds hadn't come from the direction where the guys had gone, so I was pretty sure it wasn't any of them. Even so, I was kind of worried that when I rode back out into the meadow, someone would be pointing at me and laughing. Happily, no one was.

When the whole group of riders was back in the meadow, we took one last look at the herd and then started back down the trail. We rode single file. With the horses having to work to keep their footing on the steep mountainside, most of the riders rode in silence, watching the trail and guiding their horses. Only Violet and Jace kept up a steady stream of conversation, mostly about what a wonderful saddle bronc rider Jace was and how well he had done competing in his first year at the college rodeos.

I was, as Ben would have put it, "poke-buttin' along" well behind the other riders, partly because I didn't want this ride to ever end and partly because I was trying to put some distance between me and Violet's voice. Even so, I could still hear her.

With all her jabbering, I almost didn't notice it.

Chapter 13
Caught in the Act

We were approaching the gate near the bottom of the mountain—the gate that was supposed to have been open, but wasn't—when I heard the faint sound of a cow mooing. Oddly, it wasn't coming from behind us, where we had left the herd, but seemed to originate from a distance off to the right.

That's when it clicked. I figured out what had been bothering me up on top of the mesa. I had seen one Charolais cow and her calf. Not three. Where were the other two? As I got to the gate, I remembered how much trouble we'd had getting the last few cows, including the one Charolais, to go through the gate and start up the trail. I also remembered the sound I had heard while I was off in the bushes by myself after lunch. Had we left some strays behind?

As soon as Freckles was through the gate, I turned him toward the far end of the meadow and urged him into a canter. When we reached the edge of the trees,

I spotted a trail and reined Freckles back to a walk. There was a lot of fairly fresh cow manure dotting the trail. Now I felt sure my suspicions were right, but I still couldn't see any cows through the trees. I stopped Freckles and looked back over my shoulder. We were well into the woods, and I couldn't see the meadow. Maybe I better go back, I thought to myself, because I sure didn't want to get lost.

Before I could decide, a cow mooed up ahead. A second cow answered her. I let Freckles walk a few more steps, stopping him just as I saw movement through the trees up ahead, to the right of the trail. A group of cows and their calves were milling around in a small canyon that cut back into the mountain. Two of the cows were a creamy white color. I was excited to realize I'd found the missing Charolais.

A man's voice startled me. It came from over by the cows.

"They're getting restless. I wish we had some hay or something to shut 'em up."

Another voice, a deep, raspy one that sounded oddly familiar, snapped back angrily, "Well, we don't."

That's when I saw the two men. They had their backs to me as they worked to keep the cows penned up in the little box canyon.

Freckles, who had been standing quietly, suddenly swung his head away from the cattle to look behind him. I heard footsteps. My heart pounding, I twisted around in the saddle and was relieved to see that it was Xender and Scout. In the same instant, both Xender and I raised a finger to our lips to shush each other. Then he signaled for me to follow him as he turned and headed back toward the meadow. At the edge of the trees he urged Scout into a gallop and took off across the meadow, with Freckles and me right behind him. We didn't slow down until we reached the trail that led down to the highway and, even then, we only slowed as much as we absolutely had to, to be safe. It wasn't long before we nearly ran into Ben, who was coming back up the trail on his filly.

"Where in tarnation did you two go gallivantin' off to?" he demanded. "Everyone else is halfway back to the horse trailers by now, and you two are off playin' hide-and-seek."

While I was trying to figure out what to say in the face of Ben's anger, Xender blurted out, "Old man Hillson is up there, Grandpa."

"And he's got some of our cattle!" I added

The look on Ben's face went from annoyed to startled in a mere instant. Ben asked, "You actually saw him? Where was he?"

Xender answered, "I couldn't see his face, 'cause his back was turned, but I know for a fact that I heard his voice. You can't mistake that voice. He was up there in the woods, past the far end of the first meadow. I couldn't make out exactly what he was saying. Could you, Meghan?"

They both turned toward me. "Well, I heard one man say that the cows were getting restless and he wished they had some hay to quiet them down. Then

I heard a man with a raspy, mean-sounding voice say they didn't. That's when Xender showed up, and we got out of there."

"Why did you two go over there in the first place?" asked Ben.

"I was just following her, after I saw her go off in the wrong direction," Xender said.

Ben looked at me, waiting for an explanation.

"Well, when we were riding back down the trail, it started bothering me when I realized that I had only seen one of the Charolais cows up on the mesa. And then I remembered that one of them had been stubborn about leaving the meadow when we were moving the herd up the trail. And, well, I started wondering if maybe her two buddies were still down here. That maybe they had gotten left behind because they had wandered the wrong direction into the woods away from the meadow. I mean, they haven't been up here before, so they wouldn't have known the way. I guess I thought I might see them in the woods if I took a quick detour, so, um, well I just did it without thinking. I guess I should have asked first," I said, my voice stumbling to a stop.

"Yes, you should have," Ben agreed almost absentmindedly. "How many men did you see? And how many cows?"

"There were just the two men, I think." Then I shut my eyes and pictured the little herd in the canyon. "Along with the two Charolais and their babies, there were probably five more cow-calf pairs."

"So, seven pairs altogether?" Ben asked.

"Yeah. I think so. Maybe eight. They were milling around, so it was hard to count them."

"Hillson probably has another man watching to see when we get down off the mountain," Ben said. He was silent for a moment before adding, "I'd bet dollars to donuts that there's someone sittin' down along the highway with a stock trailer and a two-way radio at this very moment."

Xender and I waited quietly while Ben pondered the options. Finally he said, "Follow me," and we headed down the trail. When we reached the highway, we saw that Mr. Searle and Mrs. Carlton were waiting for us at the trailhead with the stock trailers. The other riders already had their horses loaded into the trailers.

Ben jumped down off his filly and handed the reins to Violet. "Take care of her for me, Violet. This filly has had enough work today," he commanded in a voice that made argument impossible, even for Violet. Then he turned to Xender and said, "Climb down off yer horse and lengthen the stirrups so they'll fit me." He didn't say anything to me, so I just dismounted and waited to see what was about to happen.

Ben hurried over to where Mr. Carlton and his son were talking to Mr. Searle. A minute later, Mr. Carlton, Jace, Casey, and Cody were getting their horses back out of the trailers and putting their bridles back on.

"Load Freckles and the filly into that trailer and get in the truck with Mrs. Carlton," Ben ordered us. "She knows what to do." Then Ben jumped up on Xender's horse and led the other men and the older boys back up the mountain trail.

When we got into the truck, Mrs. Carlton told us, "Buckle up. We're going to follow Mr. Searle's truck and trailer back toward Dolores. Hopefully, whoever is helping Old Man Hillson will see us and radio to Hillson that it's safe to move the cattle they've stolen. Once we're close enough to Dolores to get cell phone coverage, we'll call the sheriff's office. Then we'll turn around and drive back to the trailhead."

I pulled my phone out of my pocket and turned it on, so I'd know when we got to an area with service.

We hadn't gone more than a mile down the highway when we rounded a curve in the road and Mrs. Carlton said excitedly, "That must be Hillson's partner in crime! Looks as if Ben was right!" As we passed him, the man was putting a little yellow two-way radio up to his ear. I took his picture on my cellphone.

A few minutes later, the truck and trailer Mr. Searle was driving moved into the wrong lane and stayed there. He didn't appear to be passing anyone, but in the distance, we could see a car coming toward him.

"What is he *doing*?" Mrs. Carlton practically screamed as she stepped on the brakes. While she was still slowing down, we saw the emergency lights start flashing on top of the oncoming car. Mrs. Carlton suddenly started laughing. "I guess that's one way to get an officer's attention." She eased the truck and trailer between Mr. Searle, who had stopped on his own side of the road, and the sheriff's car, which was now pulled off on the other side, lights blazing.

"We'll find a place to turn around," she explained. "By the time we get back, Mr. Searle will have had time to explain—I hope."

We turned around on a road that led off toward an abandoned cabin and were soon back to where the officer and Mr. Searle were just pulling back onto the highway. We waved to Mr. Searle and followed the sheriff's car up the highway. There were two officers in the car.

"Why don't they have their siren on?" asked Xender. "They're going to a crime scene!"

"Which is probably why they don't have it on," answered Mrs. Carlton. "They don't want the rustlers to know they're coming."

"Oh, yeah," said Xender.

"You're such a dork," Violet informed him.

A few minutes later, Xender pointed out, "That's the pullout where the man with the trailer was waiting."

"Yes it is," Mrs. Carlton agreed. "He probably drove to the trailhead by now."

A few minutes later, the officers pulled in next to the stock trailer, which was now backed in at the trailhead as Mrs. Carlton had predicted. She pulled in right in front of the truck, blocking it from leaving.

"You kids stay in the cab," she told us.

We did as she told us, but Xender had been quick enough to roll the window down before she cut the ignition off, so we could hear part of what was being said. It seemed to me as if everyone was being really polite, with the officers asking what the man was doing.

"Just waiting for some friends who are out trail riding," the man claimed with a fake-looking smile.

"Mind if I take a look at your two-way radio?" asked the lady officer.

"I'd be happy to show it to you, ma'am, if I had one of those," the man replied, still smiling.

"Yes, he does," shouted Xender. "Or he did, anyway! I saw him throw it into the bushes when we pulled up."

The man, still smiling, said, "The kid is mistaken, ma'am. I didn't throw anything away."

Mrs. Carlton looked back at Xender, who pointed her in the right direction. She walked over, poked around in the bushes, and then bent down and picked something up.

"That's not mine," the smiling man told the officers. "I don't own anything like that."

I quickly pulled my phone out and looked back at the picture I'd taken of him. "Mrs. Carlton," I shouted, "Come look at this!"

She came back to the truck, looked at my phone, and then carried it over to the lady officer.

"How soon will Mr. Hillson be here with the cattle?" the lady officer asked, after showing him his picture on my phone.

The man wasn't smiling anymore. "Listen, lady, none of this was my idea. I thought I was signing on for some honest work. I didn't know he was planning to rustle any cattle till we got up here."

The other officer pulled out some handcuffs. As he put them on Smiley, he started saying, "You have the right to remain silent…"

"Wow, this is just like TV!" said Violet.

Shortly, we heard the sound of cattle coming down the trail. Just after they came into view, they started to scatter as the two riders pushing them wheeled their horses around and tried to take off. Almost immediately, the riders were forced to a stop and the cattle regrouped as Ben and the rest of our crew appeared out of the woods behind them.

I heard Ol' Ben's voice. "Nice try, Hillson. You got the cows this far. We think you ought to show these nice officers how many of 'em you *almost* got away with."

Cowgirls Don't Quit

Chapter 14
A Free Horse

We got home a lot later than expected that evening. I could see that my parents didn't look too happy. They were actually waiting in Ben's driveway for us when we pulled in.

"Why didn't you call as soon as you got back into cell phone range, sweetie? We've been worrying about you," Mom asked as I got out of the truck.

I was trying to figure out a way to explain that the lady officer had taken my phone for evidence without having Mom freak out, when Ben came to my rescue.

"Well, Mrs. Callahan, I can probably explain that to you and yer husband just as soon as we get these horses taken care of. And, uh," he continued, with a completely bewildered look on his face, "does anyone know what horse that is in the round pen?"

Everyone turned to look toward the round pen, where a thin little palomino mare was trotting back and forth nervously, watching us unload the horses.

"That's Meghan's new horse," Mom said proudly.

I stopped in my tracks, staring at the horse, then back at my parents, then back at the horse, trying to figure out if Mom had just said what I thought she said.

Dad added, "We would have let you know ahead of time, Ben, but this opportunity came up rather suddenly. And you did tell us awhile back that we could keep a horse here when we got one. Anyway, a friend of one of my co-workers offered to give us a horse for Meghan. He even said he'd deliver her on the way out of town. So, here she is."

Violet snickered. "Free horse. Right. They're the most expensive kind."

I looked at Violet, annoyed, wondering why she was trying to ruin this special moment. I had a horse of my own! Then I turned to see how Xender would respond to his obnoxious sister's comment. But he was looking down at his boots as he walked past me, leading his horse to the hitching rack.

Ben said, "Let's get these horses taken care of. Then we'll talk."

My folks had just a few seconds of freak-out when Ben explained why we were late and what happened to my phone. But Ben used their excitement about giving me the horse to gloss over the cattle-rustling incident as he steered the conversation to the palomino instead. We were standing next to the round pen, watching her.

Up close, I could see that, along with being kind of skinny, her coat was dull and her mane and tail were full of dreadlocks. But with good feed and care, I just knew she was going to be really beautiful!

"Shucks, of course I meant it when I said Meghan could keep a horse here when she got one. I'm just a little surprised at coming back to the ranch and finding that horse here," Ben said.

"Well, with her birthday just two days away, it seemed like too good an opportunity to pass up, especially since the horse she usually rides has been hurt," Dad said.

"How is that horse doing?" Mom asked. "Meghan seems very fond of him. Rowdy, isn't it?"

"Yep, Rowdy. He's doin' okay," Ben answered. "He's gettin' on in years, so it may take him a little longer to heal up than it used to, but, yeah, he's doin' okay," Ben repeated.

"Well, I'm glad to hear that," Mom said.

"Now, about this new horse," Ben asked, "did they give you her health records?"

"Uh, no," Dad said. "I don't remember seeing anything like that."

"How about registration papers?"

"Well, they gave us a photocopy of his papers," Dad said, handing them to Ben.

"Her papers," Mom corrected.

"Her papers. And they said we should be able to get the originals without too much trouble."

Ben shook his head.

My parents exchanged a look.

"Back to the health records— First thing tomorrow, you will need to call all the local veterinarians' offices and see if any of them have records for this horse," Ben said. "What's the previous owner's name?" He looked at the copy of the registration papers he was still holding. "Looks like Nick Clayton. Or is it Rick Clayton?"

"That's not the name of the man who gave her to us," Dad said, reaching for the papers. "His name was Harrington, I think."

Ben looked at my parents.

My parents looked at each other.

"That's going to be a problem, isn't it?" Dad said.

"It may well be," said Ben. "I'll give you the phone number for the American Quarter Horse Association; you can call them and see if you can get it straightened out. That's going to take some time. And probably some money. But for right now, her health records need to be your first priority. This little mare is going to have to stay isolated from the rest of my horses until we know she has all of her vaccinations and until we've got a negative Coggins test on her."

My parents exchanged a look again.

Ben saw it and kept going. "I'll give you a list of the veterinary work you'll need. If you can't find out that the work has been done anywhere, you'll need to get it done for her as soon as possible. I'll give you my vet's number if you want to have her handle it."

"Thank you, Ben," Dad said. He looked over at the mare and then down at his shoes before looking back at Ben. "We kinda jumped into this without looking, didn't we?"

"Maybe," said Ben. "But I can't fault you for doing something you thought would make this girl of yours happy. She's a good kid."

I tore my gaze away from the mare long enough to look at Ben. He winked at me.

"We'll do our best to make this mare work out for her," Ben promised.

At dinner that night, I told Mom and Dad more of the fun parts about the day's adventure, skipping over the parts about the cattle thieves that I didn't think they'd appreciate. But I also admitted how sad I was that the cattle drive was over.

"You're going to miss getting up at 4:00 every morning?" Mom asked. "I'm certainly not."

"We slept in till 5:00 this morning," I reminded her. "And, yes, I'm going to miss every minute of it. Well, except for seeing Rowdy get hurt. That was kind of awful."

"Ben says he's doing better," Mom said.

"I think he is," I agreed, "but his legs are still pretty swollen. He *is* starting to move without limping as much though, so I think that means he's doing okay."

"You seem to have enjoyed riding the other horse," Mom commented.

"Freckles? Oh, he's wonderful!"

"What about your new horse?" Dad asked. "Do you think she's going to be wonderful too?"

"Oh, yes! With Ben's help, I know she will be!"

About the Author

After earning her teaching degree at Penn State University, Susan Carpenter Noble tucked it in her hip pocket and took off for Colorado to become a horse trainer. Somehow, her mentors got the gangly six-footer to where she could actually get something done on a horse, and she won state championships in such diverse events as Reining, Western Riding, and Working Hunter. She also coached students to state championships in Dressage, Trail, and Barrel Racing, among others.

When she's not out in the arena teaching her Horse Kids, or hiking with her husband, or traveling to see her far-flung siblings and adult kids, she's usually typing away on the keyboard, telling the kinds of horse stories she would like to have read growing up.

Her debut novel, *Cowgirls Don't Quit,* and the soon-to-be-released sequel, *The Free Horse,* were inspired by two of her recent students. The rest of her students are currently on their best behavior for fear she will embarrass them in a similar manner.